Fight for Your Right to Party

"Did Clyde say he thought I was cute?" Tamera asked.

"Tamera! We didn't discuss you after you left," Tia said. "But I guess he must think you look cute . . ."

"Are you serious?"

"Because you look like me, and he thinks I'm cute enough to invite to his next party."

"His next party?" Tamera shrieked. "You've been invited to one of Clyde Hemming's parties?"

Tia clamped her hand swiftly over Tamera's mouth. "Shhh. Do you want my mother to hear?"

"You're right," Tamera said in a low voice. "She'd never let you go in a million years."

Sister Sister

✿ COOL IN SCHOOL ✿

JANET QUIN-HARKIN

A MINSTREL® BOOK

Published by POCKET BOOKS
New York   London   Toronto   Sydney   Tokyo   Singapore

A MINSTREL PAPERBACK *Original*

A Minstrel Book published by
POCKET BOOKS, a division of Simon & Schuster Inc.
1230 Avenue of the Americas, New York, NY 10020

Copyright © 1996 by Paramount Pictures

ISBN: 0-671-00176-0

First Minstrel Books printing August 1996

10 9 8 7 6 5 4 3 2 1

A MINSTREL BOOK and colophon are registered trademarks of Simon & Schuster Inc.

Printed in the U.S.A.

Tamera: Hi there, I'm Tamera and this is my sister, Tia. We're identical twins.

Tia: We're having so much fun together because we only just met.

Tamera: That's because we grew up in different families. Weird, huh?

Tia: What Tamera means and isn't explaining very well is that we were split up and adopted into different families as babies.

Tamera: My dad, Ray, is kind of quiet and conservative. He runs his own limo business. He and I live in this nice big suburban house, and I've always had pretty much everything I wanted.

Tia: And I have the craziest mother in the world.

She's a struggling fashion designer. I grew up in the inner city, and it was tough.

Tamera: But now Tia and her mom have moved into our house so that we can be together.

Tia: And it's working out just great . . .

Tamera: Most of the time.

Chapter 1

൭൭

*T*amera, wait up!" Tia Landry's voice echoed down the school hall.

Tamera Campbell stopped in her tracks and spun around, surprised. It wasn't like Tia to be so loud. Usually she, Tamera, was the twin who did things like yell down school hallways. Tia was fighting her way through the crowd, her face alight with excitement. She pushed through the middle of a group of cheerleaders. A large guy's elbow almost knocked off the beret she was wearing. Instead of telling him to watch what he was doing, she just grabbed it and crammed it back onto her head as she ran.

This is serious, Tamera thought. She waited, bursting with curiosity, as her sister caught up with her.

"Tamera," Tia gasped as she finally reached her sister and clung to her shoulder, completely out of breath. "I am so excited. I can't wait to tell the whole world."

"I think you already did," Tamera said dryly as the cheerleaders passed, frowning at Tia.

"But I had to find you and tell you first," Tia went on.

"I should hope so," Tamera said. "I'd be mad if you told anyone else before me." Then she grabbed Tia and shook her. "What? What is it that you want to tell me?"

Tia shook her head as if she were still in shock. "The most amazing thing, Tamera. You'll never believe in a million years . . ."

"You got an invitation to Clyde Hemming's next party?"

Tia laughed. "Get real," she said. "Not *that* amazing. Clyde Hemming isn't going to invite you or me to one of his parties."

"Hey, speak for yourself," Tamera said. "Personally I intend to get him to notice me and start hanging out with his crowd any day now."

Tia started laughing.

"What's so funny about that?" Tamera demanded, putting her hands on her hips.

"Tamera—Clyde Hemming is the number-one sophomore hunk at this school, right?"

"Right."

"And he only hangs out with the most popular

kids? And his parties are supposed to be the coolest of the cool?"

"Right."

"I think I just proved my point," Tia said. "There is no way he'd ever invite you or me. We are definitely uncool, Tamera."

Tamera sighed. "You're right. He never even looks at people like us. He sweeps through the halls as if he owns this place. He doesn't even look in our direction—"

"Enough about Clyde Hemming," Tia interrupted. "You're getting me off track here. Don't you want to know my amazing news?"

"Of course I do," Tamera said. "Tell me, this instant."

"Okay." Tia put down her book bag and started gesturing with her hands as if she were about to make a speech. "Get this." She took a deep breath. "I have been invited to join the Einsteinettes."

Tamera looked bewildered. "The what?"

"You haven't heard of them? You know, Lady Einsteins . . . E equals mc squared?"

"They're a rap group, right?"

"No, dummy," Tia snapped. "It's a club at school—a very exclusive club. That's probably why you've never heard of it. You have to be nominated and get an invitation to join."

"Like a secret sorority, you mean?" Tamera asked. "Hey, that's cool."

"Not exactly a sorority," Tia said. "It's a science

club. It's official name is the Future Female Scientists, but the members call themselves the Einsteinettes as a joke. After Albert Einstein, you know? The guy who discovered relativity?"

Tamera wrinkled her nose. "The old guy with all the white hair?"

"That's the one."

"Let me get this straight," Tamera said slowly. "You are excited about joining a club for old guys with white hair?"

Tia laughed. "No. But he's our role model."

"You're not going to brush your hair for a week?"

"Will you get serious," Tia said. "It's an exclusive club for future female scientists. The best female brains in the school are invited to join, and we discuss topics like the Big Bang theory of the universe and prepare for college scholarships . . . that kind of thing."

There was a long pause, while students pushed past them.

"Well, go on, say something," Tia prompted.

"You're excited about this?" Tamera asked at last. "A club to talk about the Big Bang, whatever that is, and you're acting like it's tickets to a Boyz II Men concert?"

"I *am* excited," Tia said. "It's an honor, Tamera. They hardly ever invite sophomores to join. So that must prove that I'm smart, right?"

She walked ahead of Tamera to her locker and flicked open the combination lock. The locker was floor-to-ceiling books, and Tia had to push with all her strength to cram the books from her backpack into it.

"Everyone knows you're smart, Tia," Tamera said. She opened her own locker. It contained a mirror, a scarf, a spare beret, and a box of Twinkies. She put her books onto the small pile at the bottom.

"I knew I wasn't exactly a dummy," Tia said, "but I didn't realize that other people thought I was smart—smart enough to be nominated for a smart people's club."

"I'm glad it's you and not me," Tamera said. "A club like that would be about the worst punishment I could imagine. You know I'm clueless when it comes to math and science."

"Only because you've never really tried," Tia said. "I've been interested in them all my life. You were probably never encouraged. It's generally known that girls get turned off to math and science if nobody encourages them."

"My dad tried to encourage me," Tamera said. "He bought me enough educational toys. I even had stacking teething rings."

"And my mother bought me Curl and Style Barbie, so I guess that doesn't explain anything."

"Except that I'm dumb and you're smart." Tamera slammed her locker shut again and snatched up her book bag.

"Don't talk like that," Tia said, putting her arm around her twin's shoulder. "It's never too late, you know. You could be smart, too, if you studied. You'd just have to spend more time cracking those books in the library."

"The what?"

"You know, that place with all the books where you have to whisper . . . down the hall from the cafeteria?"

Tamera made a face again. "I'm allergic to libraries. They're full of geeks."

The sisters joined the stream of students, heading for the main exit.

"Tamera, I'd be happy to help you if you want to improve your math and science grades," Tia said. "As a matter of fact, I can sign up to be a tutor now that I'm an Einsteinette. I could practice my tutoring skills on you."

"Uh, thanks, but no, thanks," Tamera said. "I'm planning to get by on my looks and personality. I'll probably be a TV anchorperson while you're studying bugs under a microscope. . . ."

"Prior to winning the Nobel prize," Tia finished for her. "I wonder if I can persuade my mom to buy me a microscope. I've always wanted one . . . and a chemistry set . . . I'll need all the right equipment now that I'm an Einsteinette."

"And a pocket-size nuclear reactor maybe?"

"Get out of here." Tia shoved her sister, almost sending her crashing into a group that was walking past. They weren't just any group of kids dressed in well-worn jeans and baggy sweatshirts. They looked as if they were fashion models about to shoot a commercial for a diet soda.

"Whoa, s-sorry," Tamera stammered. "Was that an earthquake? I swear the floor just shook."

A tall girl with fashionably braided hair decorated with beads gave her a withering look and then turned back to her friends. "Some kids are so juvenile," she said, loudly enough for Tamera to hear.

Tamera was about to die of embarrassment, but suddenly she grabbed Tia's arm. "Did you see who that was? That was Clyde Hemming in the middle of that group. I almost had a chance to come into contact with him and I blew it."

"Wrong kind of contact, Tamera. I don't think you'd have made the right impression if you'd flattened him against the lockers," Tia said kindly.

"I couldn't have made any worse impression than I already have." Tamera sighed. "Now he thinks I'm a juvenile, uncoordinated weirdo."

"Yeah, I'd say that's a pretty accurate description," Tia teased. Then she saw Tamera's distressed face. "I'm sorry," she said. "I didn't realize you were serious about wanting to meet Clyde Hemming. I thought he was just a fantasy."

"I don't see why. I'm a girl and he's a guy. And I'm not exactly repulsive looking, am I?"

"No, but you're not exactly in the same league as those girls with Clyde, either."

The twins reached the exit doors and got swept through them in the tide of people.

"I don't see why not," Tamera said. "What do they have that I don't—apart from great figures, great clothes, and expensive hairdos?"

Tia laughed. "Parents who let them dress like that, for one thing. Your dad would have a fit if you tried to leave the house in a skin-tight minidress like that girl was wearing."

"You're right." Tamera sighed. "We don't have a chance with such boring, uncool parents. They never let us do anything fun."

"They'd certainly never let us go to one of Clyde's parties, so forget about him and concentrate on finding us nice, ordinary guys we can have fun with," Tia said.

"Just the girls I was looking for," came a voice right behind them.

They spun around and there, standing between them, looking very pleased with himself, was Roger, their annoying, pint-size next-door neighbor.

"Roger, what are you doing, creeping up on us like that?" Tamera demanded. "You almost made my heart stop."

Roger looked pleased with himself. "Yeah, girls have said that I make their hearts skip a beat."

"From horror, Roger," Tia said coldly. "What did you want anyway?"

"Just to offer you girls a ride home."

"But you take the school bus, just like us," Tia said, puzzled.

"I know that. What I was offering was to fight

my way onto the bus ahead of you to save you a good seat at the front."

"Roger, that's very sweet of you," Tia said cautiously. "What's the catch?"

"Just as long as you let me squeeze into the seat between you," Roger finished.

"I knew it," Tamera said. "Roger, you never get the message, do you?"

"What message?"

"That neither Tia or I would ever consider you as a potential date if you were the last guy left in the universe."

She took Tia's arm. "Come on, Tia. Let's go fight for our own seat on the bus."

They swept ahead of Roger, who was watching them with a big grin on his face.

"I think I'm finally breaking down their resistance," he said with satisfaction.

As the bus pulled out of the parking lot, a big black Camaro with fire decals on the sides cut in front of it, then took off down the street with tires screeching.

"Did you see who that was?" Tamera shrieked. "That was Clyde Hemming. He's already got his own car. Man, what doesn't he have?"

"One of us as a girlfriend?" Tia suggested with a grin.

Chapter 2

๑๑

"So what do you think, Tamera?" Tia asked.

Tamera looked up from the talk show she was watching on TV. Tia was standing in the doorway, holding up two outfits on hangers. One was a plaid skirt with a white shirt; the other was gray pants and a navy blazer.

"Which of these outfits?" Tia asked again, jiggling the hangers.

Tamera looked confused. "For what? You're thinking of going to a Catholic school or working in a bank?"

"No, silly. I'm trying to decide what to wear for my first meeting of the Einsteinettes tomorrow."

"Is one of the rules that you have to look like a geek?" Tamera asked, wrinkling her nose.

Tia frowned. "I want to make the right impression at my first meeting. I want them to know that even though I'm only a sophomore, I'm serious and dedicated in my pursuit of science and knowledge."

"I guess it doesn't matter too much what you wear in the club if there aren't any boys," Tamera said. "I think I'll go shopping at the mall tomorrow and pick out a new outfit. I want Clyde Hemming to know that I'm serious and dedicated in my pursuit of him."

Tia looked hurt. "You don't have to make fun of me, Tamera," she said. "I know that you don't think this is any big deal, but it is for me. All my life I've studied hard, and it's finally paying off. I can say to myself, if the Einsteinettes have noticed me, then good colleges will notice me. It will give me the confidence I need."

Tamera got up guiltily and went over to Tia. "I'm sorry," she said. "I *am* happy for you. And I'm proud of you, too. It will give me a great opening line at parties when you win the Nobel prize. I'll be able to say, 'Did you see the Nobel prize ceremonies? The cute one was my sister.'" Then a big smile spread across her face. "People might even mix us up. Wouldn't it be funny if people came up to me and asked me what I thought about the origin of the universe?"

"And people might think I'm you and ask me directions to the nearest mall," Tia quipped, then stopped herself. "That wasn't nice," she said. "I know you're going to do just as well as I am, Tamera. All you have to do is decide what you're interested in—besides boys—and go for it. We're twins. Those brain genes must have been divided equally."

Tamera made a face. "I think you got all the brains, and all I got was extra flab around my thighs," she said.

Tia went over to the window. "I wish my mom would come home," she said. "I'm dying to tell her the news. She's going to be so proud of me."

Tamera grinned. "Yeah, I bet she yells it around the whole neighborhood," she said. "Knowing your mom, she might even take out billboards or put an ad on a local TV channel."

Tia smiled, too. "She does get carried away sometimes, doesn't she? But I like that. I like people with spirit and enthusiasm. Your dad is so low key, he'll probably just shake my hand and say, 'Congratulations, Tia,' and that will be that."

"My dad finds it harder to express his feelings," Tamera said. "I guess guys are like that."

"Don't ask me," Tia said. "I'm not an expert on guys. The only guy I know well is Roger, and I'd hate to think he was typical." A dreamy look crossed her face. "Maybe the Einsteinettes will hold dances with the guy Future Scientists and I'll meet a brilliant, serious-yet-sensitive guy and be able to discuss my innermost feelings with him."

Tamera put her hand up to her mouth to try to stop the spluttered laugh.

"What's so funny about that?" Tia demanded. "It's good to have things in common with guys you date. That way you can talk and not get bored."

"I don't think I'd get too bored around Clyde," Tamera said. "And if you're thinking of teaming up with a future scientist, just don't ask me to double-date with you, okay?"

A door slammed and a voice yelled, "Tia, honey, I'm home!"

Tia pushed ahead of Tamera to race down the stairs. "Hi, Mom, guess what?" she yelled.

Tia's mother, Lisa Landry, was standing inside the front door, her arms full of enormous shopping bags. "Don't yell, honey," she said, dropping the bags and putting her hand up to her head. "Mama's feeling very fragile."

"What's wrong?" Tia asked, hurrying to pick up the packages for her mother. "Are you sick?"

"Sick of traveling by bus and having my toes stepped on." Lisa groaned. "I had to go clean across town to find lace to match the fabric I just bought. I thought an order to make eight bridesmaids dresses was fantastic until I tried to carry all that fabric home. I would never have believed lace could be so heavy. I've been standing on a crowded bus for over an hour, with some guy breathing down the back of my neck."

"Why didn't you tell him to back off and give you some space?" Tia asked.

"Because there wasn't room for me to turn my

head to face him," Lisa said. "But he got the message after I dug my high heel into his foot a couple of times." She laughed, then let out a weary sigh. "But now I'm ready to drop. Be an angel and make your mama a cup of tea, okay?"

"Okay," Tia said.

"And put that frozen lasagna in the oven, will you?" Lisa called. "I'm too tired to cook tonight." She started to stagger upstairs, dragging the packages with her. Tia looked after her, then went into the kitchen. Tamera followed her in.

"Oh, well, I guess my mother's not exactly dying to hear my news," she said flatly.

"Maybe now's not the right time to tell her," Tamera suggested. "Why not wait until dinner? Then you can make a big announcement and tell my dad at the same time."

Tia shrugged. "I'm beginning to think that I'm the only person who thinks this is a big deal."

"Your mom's just tired right now. Wait until she's stuffed full of lasagna. She'll be like a new woman," Tamera said. "You know she makes a big deal out of anything you do. Remember when she told the garbage man that you'd just got your first training bra?"

Tia groaned. "Don't remind me. At least this time it's something I really want the world to know." She took the lasagna from the freezer. "I thought we might have a special dinner to celebrate tonight," she said. "Somehow frozen lasagna wasn't my first choice of entrée."

"We could make a salad to go with it," Tamera said. "And there's mint chocolate chip ice cream."

"I guess it will have to do," Tia said. "It's just that somehow I pictured this a little differently."

"The Nobel prize banquet will be better," Tamera said, putting her hand on her sister's shoulder. "And you won't have to cook that yourself, either."

An hour later the lasagna was bubbling away in the oven and Tamera had set a pretty table.

"We didn't have any flowers," she said, "so I've brought down the potted plant from the bathroom."

"Gee, that makes it all very festive," Tia said dryly.

"Hey, I'm trying, I'm trying," Tamera said, irritated. "Do you want to go find a red carpet for the stairs? A crown maybe?" She paused while she put napkins on the dinner table. "It's only a club at school, Tia. You're acting like it's the Nobel prize already."

"Just because you never had anything to brag about . . ." Tia started, then stopped herself. "Sorry. I guess I'm feeling like a balloon that's been left to go flat. Maybe I did overreact to something that's really not important. I won't make any big announcement. I'll just casually let it drop in the middle of dinner, okay?"

Tamera straightened the napkins, feeling bad. Tia had been so excited, so hopeful. She had helped make Tia's balloon go flat when she should have been proud of her.

At that moment the front door opened and Ray Campbell, Tamera's father, came in.

"How are my girls?" Ray called, throwing down his briefcase onto the hall table. "What's for dinner? I'm starving."

"It's lasagna," Tamera said, going up to give her father a hug. "Tia and I fixed dinner. Lisa wasn't feeling well."

"Smells great," Ray said. "Let's eat. Is Lisa too sick to join us?"

"No, she was just exhausted from fighting her way across town on the bus," Tamera said. "I'll give her a call. Why don't you serve the lasagna, Tia?"

"Sure, that's me, the maid," Tia muttered to herself as she went into the kitchen. "The only maid in the world with a genius IQ."

Lisa hobbled down the stairs as Tia was bringing out the food. "Tia, honey, I've got an important lesson about growing up to give you," she said as she staggered to her chair.

"What?" Tia asked suspiciously.

"Never wear spiked heels when you have to travel long distance by bus," Lisa said. "My feet are killing me. My toes have swollen to the size of bananas."

"Thanks for sharing that with us when we're about to eat," Ray said, giving Tamera a wink.

"Right after dinner I'm going to go soak in a tub," Lisa said. "But maybe if I keep on getting commissions for bridesmaids dresses and move on to wedding gowns, too, I can afford to take taxis in the future. Maybe the business will get so big that I'll employ Tia as my sales manager. She's got a head for figures—right, Tia, honey?"

Tia gave a weak smile.

"What's the matter with her?" Lisa asked, looking at Tamera. "Is my baby coming down with something? She doesn't look too good."

"Tia has some big news to share," Tamera said. "She's been dying to tell you all evening, but you haven't given her a chance."

"Big news? What is it?" Lisa demanded.

Tia looked down shyly. "Maybe it's not as big as I thought it was, but I was pretty proud of it," she muttered.

"Go on. Tell us!" Lisa yelled.

Tia looked at Tamera for support. Tamera smiled encouragingly. "Go on. Tell them," she said. "I will if you don't."

"Okay," Tia said. She took a deep breath, still staring down at her lasagna, in case they weren't any more impressed than Tamera had been. "I've been invited to join a club at school," she said.

Total silence.

"Uh, that's nice, honey," Lisa said halfheartedly.

"Tell them what it's for," Tamera prompted.

"It's for future women scientists," Tia went on.

"It's very exclusive. They hardly ever invite sophomores to join. I'll be the only one this year."

"Tia, that's great," Ray said, before anyone else could say anything. "I'm really proud of you. What an honor."

"A club for brainy people?" Lisa demanded. "An exclusive club, by invitation only?"

Tia nodded. "There are only about twenty members. You have to be nominated by the science teachers. We help each other get college scholarships."

Lisa jumped up and snatched away Tia's steaming plate of lasagna.

"What are you doing?" Tia demanded.

"Getting my baby brain food," Lisa stated. "She can't eat this junky stuff. She needs fish and fresh vegetables to feed that genius brain."

"Mom, sit down," Tia said, laughing. "You are too much."

"Too much?" Lisa went on, dancing around the room now. "Honey, I always knew you were smart. I am so proud of you I could burst."

She ran to the front door and opened it. "Hey, everybody, listen up!" she yelled into the night. "My baby is one of the smartest kids in her school. She's going to Harvard or maybe Princeton or Yale's not bad. . . ."

"Mom, shut the door and stop yelling, please," Tia begged, giving her sister a despairing look.

"Hey, you, newsboy on a bike!" Lisa was still

going on. "You tell the editor at that newspaper that I've got a hot piece of breaking news for him. 'Genius in the Suburbs'—that's what he can call it."

"Mom, shut the door and sit down!" Tia insisted. "Ray, make her come inside. She's embarrassing me."

Ray got up. "Lisa. You're embarrassing her," he said, leading Lisa away and forcing the door shut. "You have every right to be proud, but there are better ways of boasting about it. The phone, for example." He fought Lisa to get at the phone first. "Okay, who do we call first? My relatives or yours? The guys at my limo company? They all know Tia. How about the principal at her old school? I bet he'd be pleased to hear—"

Lisa pushed him aside. "Let me talk first. She's my daughter."

"Mom, will you knock it off," Tia insisted, jumping up to wrestle the phone away from her mother. "No phone calls, no billboards, no messages via satellite, no carrier pigeons, okay? Just be happy for me. That's all I ask."

Ray looked at Tia fondly. "I couldn't be prouder if she were my daughter, too," he said. "Honey, you've worked hard, and you deserve all the good things that are coming to you. Those Ivy League schools are going to be fighting over you in a couple of years." He looked across at Tamera, who was the only one still sitting at the table, eating her way through a large plate of lasagna. "See, Tamera, what

I've always tried to tell you? If only you'd studied hard like your sister, you might be writing your own ticket to a good college by now."

Tamera went on eating and said nothing. She couldn't think of anything to say that wouldn't sound mean and petty, and she was happy for Tia. She just wished that everybody wasn't making such a big thing out of it.

Suddenly Ray clapped his hands together. "I've got a great idea," he said. "Let's go out to celebrate. I'm going to drive you girls in one of my limos."

Tamera and Tia ran over to Ray and flung their arms around him. "Are you serious, Dad?" Tamera shrieked. "You're going to take us somewhere in a limo?"

"That's what I said."

"Where? A fancy restaurant? A theater?" Lisa wanted to know. "Tell me what I've got to wear. I like to look right, you know."

"Let it be a surprise," Ray said. "Somewhere that's just right to celebrate Tia's success."

Half an hour later they were cruising through Detroit in a big white limo. Tia and Tamera looked out through the tinted windows and waved to people who couldn't see them.

"I bet they think that some celebrity is in here," Tia said.

"There *is* a celebrity in here," Lisa said firmly.

"My daughter, the future scientist, the smartest girl in the school."

"Mom, don't you dare roll down that window and start yelling again," Tia warned.

Ray looked at his watch. "I'd better step on it. The show starts in twenty minutes," he said.

"Ooh, so we're going to a theater then," Lisa bubbled. "I knew it! And you told us not to get too dressed up. I just hope I look good enough. Is it the orchestra or maybe a box? I've always wanted to sit in a box. What's playing? I hope it's not Shakespeare. I never could understand a word that man was saying."

"Ah. Here we are," Ray said, turning into a big parking lot. "Made it with minutes to spare."

Tia and Tamera peered out of the windows.

"Wait," Tamera said. "This isn't a theater."

Lisa got out. "Where are we?" she demanded.

Ray got out, beaming as he opened Tia's door for her. "Somewhere that's just right for a budding future scientific genius," he said. "We're just in time for the evening show at the planetarium!"

Chapter 3

ॐॐ

*T*amera turned her key and let herself into the house.

"Yoo-hoo, anybody home?" she called hopefully. Her voice echoed through the empty house. She threw down her backpack and then walked across the room to throw herself down on the sofa. She hadn't really expected anybody to be home. She knew Ray would never leave his business so early, but she had hoped that Lisa might be upstairs, starting on those bridesmaids dresses. And she felt that she needed company right now, even if Lisa still wanted to babble on about how clever Tia was.

It had been so strange, coming home all by herself on the school bus. In fact it was the first time she could remember that she and Tia hadn't ridden the bus home together since Tia and Lisa moved in with them. It wasn't that she minded taking the bus alone, or even being in the house by herself. It was knowing that Tia was at her first meeting of the Einsteinettes that bugged her.

All day long she had tried to feel pleased for Tia. She tried telling herself that being admitted to the Einsteinettes was no big deal and that nobody but a super-geek would be impressed by it. But as the day progressed, she found her spirits and self-confidence sinking lower and lower. It seemed as though everyone in the entire school knew about Tia's election to the science club. Complete strangers pointed out Tia to each other. Principal Vernon stopped the sisters as he passed them in the hall.

"This is an honor indeed, Tia," he said. Then he gave Tamera a sort of half smile that never really reached his eyes. "A little hard work on your part mightn't be a bad idea, eh, Tamera? Now that you see what there is to aim for?"

Tamera managed a weak answering smile. "Oh, sure," she muttered. "It's always been my biggest dream to be an Einsteinette—not!" she added under her breath as the principal walked away.

"How about that?" Tia grabbed her arm excitedly. "He knows my name!"

"He knows mine, too," Tamera said, wincing.

"Don't forget—I won't be taking the bus home with you today," Tia said.

"How can I forget? You've told me a million

times," Tamera snapped. "Let me guess. It couldn't be the first meeting of the Einsteinettes, could it? How clever of me. See, I'm not as stupid as I look."

Tia put her hand on her sister's shoulder. "Stop talking like that, please, Tamera. You're not stupid. And please don't be mad at me. This is the first really good thing that's happened to me in my entire life—apart from bumping into you in that clothes store."

"I'm not mad at you, Tia. I'm proud of you, too," Tamera said. "And maybe it will turn out to be a good thing for me. If seniors know your name, they'll learn my name, too, right? Maybe even Clyde Hemming will find out our names."

Tia shook her head, laughing. "I don't think that guys like Clyde Hemming are impressed by things like science clubs," she said. "He'd probably think it was totally uncool and boring."

The bell rang. "I've gotta run," Tia said. "I want to check out the latest edition of *Scientific American* from the library so I'll be well read before the meeting. See ya, Sis."

" 'Bye," Tamera said. She headed for her locker, having just remembered that she had left *Romeo and Juliet* behind. If she didn't move fast, she'd be late for English and get another tardy slip. Three tardies and her grade would be lowered, which wouldn't be the best idea, because it was already a C.

As she came around the corner, someone grabbed her arm.

"Excuse me," a deep voice said. Tamera looked up, startled, into the deep, dark eyes of James Butler, editor of the school newspaper. "I hope you don't mind."

Tamera looked up at that handsome face and decided that she'd be willing to risk a week of detention for tardiness if James Butler wanted to speak to her.

"Do you have a moment?" he asked.

Tamera's heart was beating so fast that she could hardly make herself answer, "Sure. No problem."

"I was wondering," James said, "if you'd like to write a piece for the next edition of the paper."

Tamera's heart did a complete flip-flop. Finally her hidden talents had been recognized. She might not have gotten A's on her English assignments, but the English teacher had seen that there was a budding writer behind the spelling and grammar mistakes—and the tardiness. He must have been the one who recommended her to James. Tia could keep her old science club. Now it was Tamera's chance to shine!

"You want *m-me* to write a piece for the newspaper?" Tamera stammered. "Wow. Gee, I'd love to. What would you like me to write about? Anything I like? My view of the world?"

James smiled. "Oh, just about you, that's all. How you first became interested in science, where you think it's going to lead you, what your plans are for college, research, that kind of stuff."

Tamera felt like a pricked balloon for the second time in two days. "Oh. You want my sister, not me," she said.

"Your sister?"

"Yeah. Tia. I'm Tamera. We're identical twins," Tamera said. "She's the smart one."

"Oh, I'm sorry," James said. "My mistake. Could you tell me where to find her?"

"She was heading for the library when I last saw her," Tamera said. "But I like to write. I could write a piece for your newspaper if you wanted."

James gave her a sort of half smile. "We're always happy to see submissions," he said. "Go ahead and write us a piece if you think you've got something worth saying. I can't promise anything, but we do read everything submitted."

"Yeah, thanks," Tamera said dejectedly. She walked away, almost colliding with a tall, serious-looking boy in glasses. His face lit up when he saw who she was. "Hey, aren't you—"

"No, you want my sister," Tamera snapped. "I'm nobody!"

And nobody was who she still felt like, alone in the empty house at the end of the day. When Tia had first moved in with them, Tamera had imagined that everything in her life would be wonderful from then on. They'd go through high school together, having fun and sharing their triumphs and tragedies. Tia looked like her mirror image, so she had expected that Tia would be just like her in other ways, too. She had never, for one moment, dreamed that Tia would be smarter and more popular than she was.

"Suddenly Tia's Cinderella and I feel like the ugly stepsister," Tamera muttered to herself. She got up and went to the freezer, helping herself to a big bowl of ice cream. Then she stopped and looked at it. If she started eating like this, she really would turn into the ugly sister. She'd be a blimp in no time at all. And if she was going to have to get by on her looks, that would be bad news.

Then another horrible thought struck her—Tia had the same looks. Whatever Tamera did, Tia would always be one step better than her, pretty and smart, too.

"Doomed," Tamera muttered to herself.

She jumped as the doorbell rang. "Obviously Bryant Gumbel coming to interview Tia," she said to herself as she crossed the living room. She opened the door and Roger walked in. In his hands were various bottles and jars.

"Where is she?" he demanded. "Where is my little genius love? I've just come to tell her that in Pythagoras's theorem, the square of the hypotenuse equals the sum of the squares of the other two sides. I don't suppose she ever realized that I was one of the undiscovered scientific brains of our time. I thought we could spend an enchanted evening doing experiments together."

"She's not here, Roger," Tamera cut in. "She's at a meeting of her science club."

"Oh," Roger said. He dumped the science equipment on the coffee table. "In that case, Tamera, how about spending an exciting afternoon at the mall with me, shopping."

Tamera opened the front door. "Roger, get lost," she said coldly.

"I can tell when I'm not wanted," Roger said. "Now, if Tia were here, there would be a meeting of the minds."

"There will be a meeting of boot against backside if you don't get out!" Tamera yelled. Roger gave her a worried look and fled.

On his way down the front path, he bumped into Lisa, her hands full of packages again.

"Hey, Mrs. Landry," he called. "I just came to pay homage to your genius daughter."

"Forget it, Roger, you're not smart enough for her," Lisa said calmly. "I only let her date honor roll students." She swept on into the house. "Is my baby home yet?" she asked Tamera.

"No, she's still at her Einsteinettes meeting," Tamera said.

"I wish she'd hurry up," Lisa said, putting her packages onto the table. "I can't wait to show her what I bought for her."

"What?" Tamera ran over excitedly. She loved getting new clothes. Tia always traded with her, so they had double wardrobes.

Lisa started emptying packages onto the table. "I went to the college store, but I couldn't make up my mind," she said.

The whole table was covered in college sweatshirts. "Which one do you think?" she started holding up sweatshirts: Harvard, Princeton, Howard, Georgetown, Yale . . .

"I kind of favor Harvard myself," she went on excitedly. "Then I can tell everyone my daughter's at Haavaad. I love saying that word. Haavaad! So elegant, don't you think?"

Tamera moved away from the pile of sweatshirts, disgusted.

"What's the matter, honey?" Lisa called after her. "Are you sad that I didn't get you anything? You can wear the ones she doesn't want."

"Thanks, but I don't intend to make myself look stupid," Tamera said. "How can I wear an Ivy League shirt when everyone knows that the only Ivy League I'd ever be in is if I worked for a flower shop."

Lisa came around to her and took her into her arms. "Don't talk like that, Tamera, honey," she said softly. "We can't all have the same talents."

"Just tell me what talents I do have," Tamera said, shrugging her off.

"You're pretty, you're vivacious, you're fun," Lisa said.

"Yeah, right," Tamera said, "and tell me which

colleges recruit people because they're pretty and fun."

"You could win Miss America—or you could marry a rich guy. Then you wouldn't need to go to college," Lisa said. "Or you could become a fashion designer, like me."

"Thanks, but I like to eat regularly," Tamera snapped.

"Hey, I'm just starting out," Lisa said. "All artists have to suffer to begin with. Look at Van Gogh. He didn't sell a painting until he was dead."

"I think that proves my point, Lisa," Tamera said, finding she was laughing. It was impossible to stay down too long when Tia's mother was around.

"Who'd want to be like him, anyway," Lisa said. "He cut off his ear. My head would feel unbalanced if I could only wear one earring." She looked at Tamera with understanding. "But what I'm saying is important, Tamera. I'm trying to follow my dream. You have to do the same."

"If I knew what my dream was," Tamera said.

"You will, honey," Lisa said. "You'll find something you love more than anything else in the world, and then you'll go for it. It's just a matter of—" She broke off as she heard a car door slam and then footsteps running toward the house.

"That has to be her now!" Lisa exclaimed as the front door burst open. "Tia, honey, you're home! How is Mama's little genius?"

For a second Tamera hoped that Tia would say

the Einsteinettes were boring or snobby and she didn't want to join the club after all. But Tia's face was glowing with happiness.

"Oh, Mom, it was fantastic," she said. "You don't know what it was like to be in a room full of people who didn't think I was a weirdo for talking about science," she said. "And a senior gave me a ride home in her car . . . and we're going to help the little kids at the elementary school get ready for their science fair . . . and best of all, guess what? I made a great new friend. Her name's Heather, and we hit it off right away. We like all the same things, and I'm going over to her house after school tomorrow night so that we can study together. Isn't that fantastic?"

"I'm so happy for you, baby," Lisa said.

"Yeah, me, too," Tamera added in a flat voice.

Chapter 4

@@

"Are you sure your family won't mind if I come over without warning them first?" Heather Braunschweiger asked Tia as they walked up the street toward Tia's house.

Tia grinned. "Heather, families freak out if you bring home friends with pierced body parts, not people like you," she said, looking at Heather's neatly braided hair, her wire-rimmed glasses, and her pleated skirt. "You have to be the sort of friend every parent wants their child to have. And besides, my family's not like that. They're really cool about stuff."

"I was thinking more about your sister," Heather said. "I wouldn't want to disturb her homework."

Tia spluttered. "My sister? She's not the world's greatest student," she said. "If she does any home-

34

work, it's on the bus going to school in the morning, usually copied from me. Tamera's one aim is to get through life having fun and doing as little work as possible."

Heather's eyes opened wide. "How terrible for you, to be stuck with a sister like that," she said. "I'm so glad I'm an only child so I don't have to put up with any sibling problems."

Tia was feeling odd. She liked Heather, and she was glad to have her for a friend, but she didn't like to hear her bad-mouthing Tamera. Also she was feeling guilty because she was the one who had started running down her sister, even if everything she had said was true.

"Oh, don't get me wrong," she said hastily. "Tamera's a great sister. We have the most fun together. It's just that she's not—" Tia was going to say smart, but she stopped herself. "She thinks there's more to life than studying," she finished. "My mother's the same way," she added. "It's funny how much she and Tamera have in common."

Heather looked puzzled. "Why shouldn't your sister take after your mother?"

"Because she's not *her* mother, too."

"Excuse me?" Heather looked bewildered. "Aren't you two identical twins?"

"Uh-huh." Tia smiled at Heather's puzzled face.

Heather shook her head. "Then it's scientifically impossible for you to have two different mothers."

"We were adopted into different families,

Heather," Tia said. "Tamera and I only met last year. And you know what's weird? My mom and Tamera like to laugh a lot. Tamera's dad is serious and interested in studying, just like me. We were given to the wrong families."

"How interesting," Heather said. "That goes against a scientific theory. Nature versus nurture? You've heard about that?"

"Oh . . . uh . . . sure," Tia lied. Heather had read so many more books than she had. She knew about everything.

"Well, here we are," Tia said, putting her key in the front door. "Hi, anybody home?"

Lisa appeared from the kitchen with Tamera right behind her, holding a bowl of ice cream in one hand.

"I've brought someone I'd like you to meet," Tia said proudly. "This is Heather. She's come over so that we can pool ideas for the little kids' science fair."

"Nice to meet you, Heather," Lisa said warmly. "Tia's told us so much about you."

"Nonstop for two days," Tamera muttered, not quite loud enough for Heather to hear.

Tia heard, though. She glared at her sister. "Heather was worried she might disturb your studying," she said with a phony laugh. "Isn't that the funniest thing? I told her that you always do your homework on the bus going to school in the morning."

"I do not!"

"Okay, so sometimes you do it in homeroom, before first period," Tia said, glancing at Heather as if she'd said something witty.

"And I was just saying to Tia how interesting it was that you were raised in a family where academics were important and Tia was raised by a mother who . . ." Heather paused, searching for the right word.

"Who grew up in the school of hard knocks?" Lisa finished for her. "Just because I didn't get chances myself doesn't mean I don't want them for my baby. I'm so proud of her, getting into this science club. I've told everyone I meet. I told the whole number thirty-seven bus yesterday."

"We're going to work up in our bedroom," Tia said, "if that's okay with you, Tamera?"

"Me? Why wouldn't it be okay with me?" Tamera said breezily. "You've already told Heather that I never do any homework. I'll just be down here, pigging out and watching talk shows like always."

Tia shot her a worried look. It wasn't like Tamera to put herself down. Usually she was the one who thought that she was great at everything.

Lisa sensed the tension and clapped her hands. "So, are you planning to stay for dinner, Heather? We're having hamburgers."

"Hamburgers?" Heather sounded shocked. "We never eat hamburgers anymore. They destroy the rain forest."

"My hamburgers come from a rain forest?" Lisa

sounded amazed. "I thought they just came from plain old cows."

Heather and Tia looked at each other and burst out laughing.

"Maybe the beef you buy at the store is raised here in the U.S.A., Mrs. Landry, but the beef that the big hamburger chains use comes from South America," Heather explained, "and they have to cut down rain forest to provide grazing for the cattle."

"Heather's family is vegetarian now," Tia said.

"In protest about the uncivilized way they kill defenseless animals," Heather said. "And also because it's the best way to save the planet."

"I want to save the planet, too," Lisa said, "but I'm not living on broccoli to do it."

"Me, neither," Tamera said. She put down her ice-cream bowl. "And since I can't get into my bedroom to do my homework, I think I'll go see if Roger wants to go to the mall with me. I heard that Clyde Hemming and his friends sometimes hang out at that new espresso bar."

She walked across to the mirror and took her brush and hairspray from her purse.

"What are you doing, Tamera?" Tia asked.

"What does it look like? Spraying my hair," Tamera answered.

"Don't you know that hairspray is destroying the ozone layer?" Heather said with annoying patience.

"Well, excuse me," Tamera snapped. "Maybe I'll

just run ozone over my hair to stop it from flying away."

"It's very serious, Tamera," Tia said. "If the ozone layer goes, there's nothing to stop all those harmful rays from zapping the earth. Right, Heather? We'll all wind up with skin cancer."

"Well, thank you, Ms. Cheerful," Tamera said. "Any more good news for us today? How's the pollution level? Are we going to die of carbon monoxide poisoning?"

"That's what scientists are for," Tia said. "At the Einsteinettes meeting they told us that our job was to monitor our planet and warn ordinary people."

"Like me," Tamera finished for her. "Thanks for reminding me how ordinary I am." She snatched up her backpack and went out the front door.

"Sorry about that, Heather," Tia said. "My sister's been acting really weird since I joined the Einsteinettes."

"It's sibling rivalry," Heather said. "She's feeling threatened by your success."

"That can't be right," Tia said. "Tamera would never want to join a science club, would she, Mom? And she said she was happy for me."

Lisa came over and put her arm around Tia's shoulder. "Tamera's just trying to find out where she belongs, that's all. She'll get over it," she said. "Just cool it with the rain forests and ozone layers, okay? Now, if you'll excuse me, I've got a date with a murdered cow in the kitchen."

Chapter 5

ॐॐ

*A*re you coming to lunch, Tia?" Tamera called as she watched her sister sprinting in the other direction down the school hall.

Tia spun around. "Oh, sorry, Tamera, I meant to tell you," she said. "I'm eating lunch with Heather."

"Again?" Tamera demanded. "That makes four days in a row."

"So? Is there any rule that says I can't eat lunch with the same person?" Tia asked defensively.

What about me? Tamera wanted to say, but even in her head it sounded childish. Tia seemed to guess what she was thinking, because she said, "Look, Tamera, just because we're twins doesn't mean we have to do everything together, does it? In fact, Heather showed me an article in *Psychology Today* that said that twins should be encouraged to grow up as individuals. It said that twins who are always dressed alike and do things together have more psychological problems as adults.

Tamera tossed back her hair. "Hey, who said I wanted to eat lunch with you?" she said. "All I was worried about was that there was only one bag of chips left this morning and you took it. I was expecting to share at lunch."

Tia rummaged into her lunch bag. "If you want it, take it," she said. "Do you know how much fat there is in a packet of chips? Heather's family is trying to cut out foods with preservatives and fat in them."

"And they've stopped breathing so they can save the ozone layer?" Tamera asked sweetly.

"Hey, Tia!"

Tia spun around as she heard her name being called. Heather was standing at the far end of the hall, holding a big pile of books.

"Your sister geek is looking for you," Tamera muttered to her sister as Heather came down the hall toward them.

"That's not nice, Tamera," Tia snapped. "Heather's a fun person when you get to know her. She's very smart."

"Tia, I thought you said we'd meet in the library," Heather called. "Weren't we going to look up that article on DNA in *Scientific American?*"

"Sorry, Heather. I got delayed," Tia called back. "See ya, Tamera," she added, and ran down the hall.

Tamera stood there, scowling at Tia's back. "Saving the ozone layer. DNA. *Scientific American.* What fun, what a blast," she muttered to herself in an imitation of Heather's crisp, prissy voice.

"Hey, Tamera, what's up?" Someone tapped her on the shoulder. Tamera turned to see it was her friend Sarah. "What are you doing just standing there in the middle of the hall?" Sarah asked with a grin. "I hope I didn't interrupt a vision or something."

"More like a nightmare," Tamera said. "My sister has been zapped into a geeky Twilight Zone."

Sarah's grin spread. "Oh, yeah, I heard about that. She joined that snobby science club, right?"

"Right," Tamera said. "And now all she can talk about is boring stuff like saving the ozone layer and the rain forest. And she's always heading for the library with that nerdy Heather."

"She'll get over it," Sarah said. "All the publicity has gone to her head right now. Give her a week or so and she'll be back to normal."

"I hope so," Tamera said. "I'm getting scared, Sarah. I mean, what if this is the real Tia and it took the science club to bring her out? What if I'm stuck sharing a bedroom with a brain and three million test tubes? What if she starts cloning my DNA while I'm asleep?"

Sarah started laughing. "I think you're freaking

out over nothing, Tamera," she said. "I know Tia, and I'd say she was as normal as you or me. I think she's just acting the part right now." She glanced at her watch. "I gotta run. I'll be late for play rehearsal."

"You're in the school play?"

"Just a drama club play. Nothing major, and I've got a small part, but it's fun. We just started rehearsals this week."

"Do you think they have any parts still open?" Tamera asked hopefully.

"I don't know," Sarah said. "Why, were you thinking of joining the drama club?"

"I need to do something," Tamera confessed. "All we talk about at home is Tia, Tia, Tia. I'd like to do something that makes people notice me, too."

"I can understand that," Sarah said. "Why don't you come down to the auditorium with me, and we can ask the director if any parts are still open."

"Okay, I will," Tamera said. She walked beside Sarah, feeling more hopeful by the minute. When they saw her act, they'd give her the lead in the play. Even if it was already filled, they'd tell the original girl that they'd made a mistake and she could now be Tamera's understudy.

She swept into the auditorium already feeling like a star. Let's see who Ray and Lisa think is more important now, she told herself. The sister in the science club discussing the boring ozone layer or the sister who steals the show in the play.

Sarah grabbed her arm. "Come on, I'll introduce you to the director," she said. Tamera put on her biggest, brightest smile as Sarah dragged her across the auditorium to where a group of seniors was standing together.

"Brad," Sarah said cautiously. "I'd like you to meet my friend Tamera."

Brad glanced up from his script. "Hi, Tamera," he said without much interest.

"Tamera wants to be in the play," Sarah said.

"Tryouts were last week," Brad said. "They were posted on the notice boards."

"I know," Tamera said, "but I wasn't sure I could fit the play into my busy schedule then. Now I've decided I made a mistake. I do want to be in it— so I wondered if you have any parts not filled yet."

"There is one," Brad said slowly.

"There is?"

"Yeah, and it's a pretty big part, too."

"It is?" Tamera's eyes opened wider and wider.

"You'd be onstage for the whole first act, and you'd have only one line to learn."

"I would?"

"Yeah. Do you think you could do it? The line is 'Moooo.' "

" 'Moooo'?"

Brad was grinning now. "Yeah. It's the cow. We don't have anyone to play the cow yet."

"The cow?" Tamera looked around. All the other

seniors were grinning, too, as if Brad had made a good joke. "You want me to play a cow?"

Brad spread his hands. "Great exposure," he said. "Of course, you'd be hidden under a cow suit, but it could be fun."

"Thanks, but I never saw myself as a budding cow," Tamera said in disappointment. "You don't have any human roles left?"

"The whole play is already cast," Brad said. "Of course we still need lots of people to paint scenery and build sets, if you're interested."

Painting scenery wasn't what Tamera had in mind. She couldn't see anyone at home getting excited about that news.

"Uh, no, thanks," she said. "I'm a lousy painter. I drip. And I can't hammer a nail without banging my thumb, either. But thanks for the offer. Next time, maybe."

Then she pushed through the group of seniors and made for the door. She was sure they were all laughing at her. She felt stupid and mad.

I'll show them, she thought. I'll find something I can shine at.

Instead of going to the cafeteria, she went to look at the notice boards along the main hallway. Notices of all the clubs and sports teams were posted there.

Okay, there has to be something here for me, she told herself as she started reading the notices. Football—that was out. Cheerleading was out, too. They had held tryouts weeks ago. Besides, she had never managed to do a cartwheel when she took gymnastics.

Swim team? She paused beside that board. She knew how to swim pretty well, didn't she? Maybe she could become a champion swimmer. And think of all those guys in cute little Speedos, she reminded herself. That would be an added bonus. Tia would definitely be jealous if her sister started dating a swimming hunk.

She didn't wait a second longer but marched in the direction of the coaches' office behind the gym. Somebody there would know where she had to sign up for swim team.

Mr. Peters, her P.E. teacher, was sitting at a desk in the coaches' office. He looked up from the form he was filling out as she came in.

"Hi, Tamera," he said. "What do you need? Have you brought in another excuse slip for P.E.?"

"No," Tamera said, hurt that he thought of her as one of those girls who was always trying to get out of P.E. classes. "I've come to sign up for swim team."

Mr. Peters looked surprised. "Great. I didn't know you were a swimmer."

"I've never been on a team before," Tamera said. "But I'd like to give it a shot. When can I start?"

"Tomorrow morning if you like," Mr. Peters said. "Six o'clock, here at the pool."

"Excuse me?" Tamera didn't think she'd heard right. "Did you say six o'clock?"

A smile spread across Mr. Peters's face. "That's right. Morning practice is from six until eight. Afternoon practice from three to five-thirty. We usually do about four thousand yards per practice."

"I, uh, think I've changed my mind," Tamera said. "Too much water is bad for a person. I get shriveled fingers just from sitting in the bathtub at home. I really don't want to end up looking like a prune. Sorry to take up your time. Gotta run." She turned and fled from the office, her heart still pounding. What a narrow escape. There were limits to what she'd do to become more famous than Tia, and they didn't include getting into cold water at six o'clock in the morning.

That afternoon, while the history teacher droned on about the ancient Romans, Tamera stared out the window, thinking hard. Out of the corner of her eye she noticed Tia's hand go up to answer yet another question. She had always known Tia was smart, but since she'd been chosen for the science club, she seemed to have blossomed into a super brain—and a real teacher's pet, Tamera thought angrily.

She drew heavy black doodles around the edge of her notebook. What can I do? she asked herself. There had to be lots of fun clubs in school. There were so many things she hadn't tried and might be good at. Then she remembered the school newspaper. James had promised to read anything she wrote, hadn't he? Maybe she could dazzle the whole school with her brilliance and wit. She chewed on her pencil and stared out the window again. It would need to be something clever and shocking to get everyone's attention.

What do I know about that's clever and shocking? she asked herself. Her mind went blank. About the most shocking thing that had happened to her was the time someone stole her lunch. Hardly the start for a great exposé! She wasn't even an expert on dating and boy-girl relationships. I've been too sheltered, she thought. It's all my dad's fault. He's protected me too much. Maybe if I'd grown up in the city like Tia, I'd know about stuff that makes good stories. All I know about is shopping and Saturday morning cartoons and limo driving.

"Tamera!" Tia whispered.

"What?" Tamera came back to the present with a jolt. She was conscious that all eyes in the classroom were on her.

"So what's your answer, Tamera?" the teacher asked with cold patience.

Tamera shot a helpless glance at Tia. She didn't even know what the question was.

"Caesar," Tia mouthed.

"What?" Tamera hadn't a clue what the teacher had been talking about.

"Caesar," Tia mouthed again.

"He wanted to seize her?" Tamera said.

The class broke out in noisy laughter.

"I don't think you've heard one word that I said today, Tamera," the teacher said. "I've been talking about Julius Caesar and his conquest of Europe. Why don't you bring me a one-page report on Caesar's life tomorrow. That way I'll know you haven't missed anything we covered today."

"Great," Tamera muttered. It felt as if she was being sucked deeper and deeper into a nightmare. Everything Tia did turned out better and better. Everything she did turned out wrong.

Chapter 6

ᏬᎧ

Tamera stood alone, clutching a tray of food while the noise echoed from the cafeteria walls and washed over her. Ever since Tia had started spending her lunch breaks with Heather, Tamera had felt uneasy. She kept telling herself that she had survived perfectly well for fourteen years without a sister. She had been popular and had friends all her life, so why was she worried now? She looked around the cafeteria and didn't see anyone she knew. Where was everybody? She began to wonder if she had been zapped into a school in a parallel universe.

"Over here, Tamera!" a voice yelled. Someone was waving in the far corner.

Gratefully she fought her way across to a table

filled with her friends Sarah, Michelle, Chantal, and Francine.

"We managed to get a table where we're not likely to get chili dropped down the back of our necks for once," Michelle said. She patted a seat beside her. "Scoot over, Sarah. Tamera can sit beside me."

"Thanks," Tamera said, squeezing in between Michelle and Sarah.

"Where's Tia?" Sarah asked. "I haven't seen her all week."

"She's probably working on a formula to patch up the ozone layer," Tamera said.

Francine looked across at Tamera and wrinkled her nose. "Sounds like she's taking this science club thing pretty seriously."

"You wouldn't recognize her," Tamera said. "She's hanging out with her fellow future scientists, planning how to save the world."

Michelle made a face. "Sounds like a lot of fun, huh? Why don't we all go and sign up for that club."

"Because you have to be a genius, Michelle," Chantal said, flipping back her long black hair. "And I don't think any of us qualifies."

Tamera didn't want to start talking about Tia and how smart she was.

"No play practice today?" she asked Sarah.

Sarah shook her head. "It's act one today. I'm only in act two," she said. "I'm sorry it didn't work out for you yesterday. I guess you didn't see yourself as a cow."

"A cow?" Francine leaned across the table. "What's this about a cow?"

Tamera made a face. "The only part still left open in the play was a cow. Somehow that didn't seem a good route to stardom. Especially since nobody would know it was me under the cow suit."

The girls at the table laughed, and Tamera laughed with them. It felt good to be the center of attention for once, surrounded by people who were interested in her.

"I didn't know you were a budding actor, Tamera," Michelle said. "You've never tried out for a play before, have you?"

"It was just a thought," Tamera said. "Everyone's making a big fuss of Tia for being Miss Scientific Genius, so I thought I'd find something I could do brilliantly."

"Flirt?" Francine suggested.

"Come up with great excuses for not doing your homework?" Michelle added.

"Come on, guys. Cut it out," Tamera said. "There must be something I can do as well as Tia. Sports teams are out, because they expect you to practice every day. And anyway, I'm not a standout at any sport. I'd probably wind up sitting on a bench most of the time. I looked at the clubs yesterday, but I couldn't think of anything that really excites me." She stuck a straw into her drink. "You're in the marching band, aren't you, Michelle? That might be kind of fun, and I'd look good in a uniform."

"I didn't know you played an instrument, Tamera," Michelle said.

"I don't, but I could fake it. With all those trumpets and trombones blasting away, who's going to know whether I'm playing or not?"

"Tamera!" Michelle said, laughing, "You are something else. You have to try out for the marching band. The music teacher has to see how well you read music and play your instrument."

"Okay, so I could play the triangle," Tamera said. "You don't have a triangle player, do you?"

"You think your family is going to be impressed with playing the triangle, Tamera?" Sarah asked.

"Maybe not," Tamera agreed. "But it could be fun to be in the marching band, and it would be a good way to meet guys, wouldn't it? I've seen some of those band guys, and they look cute in their uniforms. When I start dating a hunky trombone player, then Tia will be impressed."

"What's with you, Tamera?" Chantal asked. "You're always so cool and laid back. And you've never had problems meeting guys, either."

"I know," Tamera said. "But I've been trying to come up with things I do better than Tia. I figured if I started dating a real trophy guy, one of the school megahunks, everyone would have to be impressed, right?"

"I don't see why you're so worried about impressing your family and Tia," Sarah said. "You guys have never been competitive before."

"My dad and Tia's mom have never treated Tia like Miss Scientific Genius before. They're positively drooling over her all the time. 'Oh, Tia, we're so proud of you. You're so clever. Here, have another Harvard sweatshirt. Let's go to the planetarium again. Get out of Tia's way, Tamera. You don't matter, because you're stupid.'"

"Oh, come on, Tamera," Sarah said. "I've been to your house, and I can't imagine your dad putting you down. He does everything to encourage you."

"Well, he's not encouraging me right now," Tamera agreed. "He keeps on saying things like 'If only you studied as hard as Tia, you could think of going to a good college some day, too.' I don't exactly find that encouraging."

"I don't know why you're getting so upset, Tamera," Chantal said. "I'd never have thought you were the kind of person who'd want to be known as a scientific genius."

"And you wouldn't really want to join that Future Female Scientists club, would you?" Francine added.

"Are you serious?" Tamera laughed. "I'd rather go to the dentist."

"So why are you letting it bug you?" Michelle said.

"Because Tia's suddenly a celebrity, I guess. Everyone in school knows who she is. She's a somebody and I'm a nobody."

"Serial killers make the headlines, Tamera," Sarah said. "Everyone knows who they are. But that doesn't mean you want to be one. So Tia's famous around school right now. But for what? Being in the nerdiest club in the school?"

Francine started giggling. "Yeah, Tamera. It's not exactly a glamour society, is it? Have you seen the way those girls dress? They look like they stepped out of a nineteen fifties sitcom."

"And how many of them date cute guys?" Michelle was laughing, too. "I bet their idea of having fun is looking at mold growing under a microscope."

"And they get excited when the college bookstore has a sale."

"Or there's a special on spiders on the public TV channel!"

Suddenly Tamera was feeling much better. Maybe joining that club wasn't such a hot thing to do after all, she thought. Her friends thought it was pretty geeky. She started laughing with them.

"You should see this Heather girl that Tia's hanging out with now," she said. "She told me that I shouldn't use hairspray because I was destroying the ozone layer."

"She did what?" Michelle chuckled. "How stupid. Everyone needs to spray their hair, especially when it's windy like this."

"Not Heather," Tamera said with a big grin. "She has a 'do from the Dark Ages. You know, one braid down her back, just like Heidi or something."

Sarah elbowed her in the side. "Is that her now, standing next to Tia?" she asked.

Tamera looked in the direction Sarah was pointing. Tia had just come into the cafeteria. Heather was standing beside her, searching around with a worried look on her face. Obviously there were no more tables free. As they watched, Heather pushed her glasses up on her nose and muttered something to Tia. At that moment Tia spotted her sister. Any other time Tamera would have called Tia over and made room for her, but there was no way she was having snobby, boring Heather at the table with her friends.

"See, what did I tell you?"' Tamera asked. "Isn't she something else?"

"Yeah, and I'm not sure what," Michelle said.

"I'm sure Heather could tell you the Latin name for the species she is," Tamera said. "*Boringus geekus* probably."

The other girls at the table laughed. "That's good, Tamera," Sarah said, giving her a high five.

"You should have heard the way she told Tia's mom that it was wrong to eat beef," Tamera went on.

"Wrong to eat beef?" Michelle asked.

"Yes, because it's destroying our planet," Tamera said, giving a very good imitation of Heather. "All the rain forests will be gone, and my hairspray will have wrecked the ozone layer. . . ."

The girls were laughing loudly now. Tamera

caught Tia's eye. For a second they stared at each other, then Tia muttered something to Heather, and they walked out of the cafeteria again.

"Nice outfit." Chantal giggled. "I hear button-down collars are really in fashion this year."

"And what has Tia done to herself?" Michelle asked Tamera. "She always looks so hip. But she looks different with her hair tied back. I liked her hair the way it was."

"And was that a pleated skirt she's wearing?" Francine asked with exaggerated horror.

Tamera grinned. "She's trying to dress like a future scientist," she said.

"She's trying to dress like a nerd," Chantal said bluntly. "You'd better get her to wise up, Tamera, or normal people won't want to hang out with her."

"Yeah, Tamera," Francine added. "Tell her that it's fine and dandy to be smart and it's okay to want to be a future scientist, but it doesn't mean you have to look like a dork and hang out with dorky people."

"Don't worry," Tamera said, a big grin spreading across her face. "I'll tell her."

When the bell rang for the end of lunch, Tamera was feeling better than she had in days. Ray and Lisa might think that Tia was wonderful. Tia might think that Tia was wonderful. But their friends at school didn't think she was so hot. Suddenly Tamera realized that she had the perfect way to get even with Tia.

Chapter 7

❀❀

Tamera was curled up on the couch, eating ice cream and watching TV when Tia let herself into the house that afternoon. It occurred to Tia that Tamera seemed to be watching a lot of TV and eating a lot of ice cream lately. She hoped that Tamera wasn't turning into a full-blown couch potato. She hoped even more that all this eating ice cream and watching TV wasn't something to do with her own new fame. Several times now Tamera had made jokes about being dumb. Tia hoped they were just jokes and that Tamera wasn't really trying to act like a dumb person.

"Hi, Sis," Tia called. "What's happening?"

"Nothing much," Tamera said. "What are you doing home? No atoms to split this afternoon? No rain forest to save?"

"I've got a ton of homework," Tia said. "So has Heather." She perched on the arm of the sofa. "That ice cream looks good."

"You wouldn't want any," Tamera said. "It's full of fat and preservatives. Heather wouldn't approve."

"I'll take the risk for once. I'm starving," Tia said, and headed for the kitchen. "By the way," she called back to Tamera, "I saw you guys in the cafeteria today. You looked like you were having a good time. What was so funny?"

"You were," Tamera said bluntly.

"Excuse me?" Tia spun around.

"We were laughing at you," Tamera said.

"Well, thanks a lot," Tia said, a hurt look spreading across her face. "Some friends you guys are."

"Sorry, Tia, but we couldn't help it. It was the way you and Heather looked. We had to laugh."

"I don't see what was so funny about Heather and me," Tia said angrily.

"Have you seen yourself in the mirror lately?" Tamera asked. "You're starting to turn into a Heather clone."

"What's so bad about that?"

"Tia, get real," Tamera said. "Heather is probably the most boring person in the universe. Why would you want to look like her?"

"I want the girls in the science club to think I'm serious," Tia said. "Besides, I might like this look."

"You're joking, right?" Tamera said, putting her hand to her mouth to stifle a laugh. "Tia, you look terrible. You used to look so good. You have now taken over as Queen of the Geeks."

"Say what you like! I don't care," Tia said. "You're all just jealous."

"Of what?" Tamera demanded.

"That I'm an Einsteinette and I'm famous at school?"

"Of being elected to a dorky club? So it proves you're super smart. We all know that. But is that how you really want to be known around school? Tia the great brain? The future scientist? The super-geek? It's not exactly cool, is it It's hardly going to attract cute guys." She got up and followed Tia into the kitchen.

"There's more to life than cute guys," Tia said.

"Yeah. Like what?" Tamera grinned. "You know what the girls said at lunch today? They said they wouldn't want to be seen hanging out with you looking like that. It would be bad for their image."

"So?" Tia demanded. "Maybe I wouldn't want to be seen hanging out with them. It would be bad for *my* image."

"Fine, if that's the way you feel about it," Tamera said. "If you want to go through the rest of high school alone with your dorky friends in that dusty old library. Personally I'm looking forward to dating fun guys, going to fun parties, and having a blast. There's time enough to be serious and boring when we grow up someday." She came up behind her sister. "You know what I think? I think you've let this dumb club go to your head. You used to be a fun person, Tia. People liked to hang out with you. Don't blow it."

"Thanks for your advice, Ms. Airhead," Tia said coldly. "Did it ever occur to you that I might like who I am now? That I might have discovered my niche?"

"I'm sure glad it's not my niche," Tamera said.

"Then I guess our paths won't be crossing too much in the future," Tia said.

"You can wave at me from the library window when I ride past in Clyde Hemming's black Camaro," Tamera said, running her fingers through her hair.

"I don't know where you get this fantasy that someone like Clyde Hemming will notice you someday," Tia said. "We look alike, Tamera. If I'm boring and ordinary, then so are you."

"It's a question of personality, Tia," Tamera said patiently. "We might look alike, but my personality is bubbling over with fun, and yours is bubbling over with something out of a test tube."

With that remark she swept out of the room and up the stairs, leaving Tia staring after her. Stupid, Tia thought. What do I care what she thinks? She's not as smart as me.

She opened the freezer, got out the ice cream, read the fat content, then hastily put it back. What did Tamera know about anything? Tia was having a good time with her new friends. It was great to be respected as a super-brain at school. It was great to be able to talk about intelligent things, instead of dumb stuff like shopping and CDs and boyfriends.

She walked over to the mirror and studied herself. With her hair pulled back from her face into a scrunchie, she looked quite different from Tamera, and younger, too. About eleven years old, in fact.

"Let her think what she likes, I don't care," she said out loud to the Tia in the mirror. But then suddenly she ripped the scrunchie out of her hair and shook it loose. The problem was that she did care. She didn't want Tamera to be the pretty and popular one. She didn't want to be known as the dorky twin.

Tamera appeared again at the top of the stairs. She was wearing her funky beret and a big crocheted purple vest over tight black jeans and a yellow T-shirt. Tia had to admit that she looked very good.

"I'm going to hang out with Sarah," Tamera said. "We might go to a movie. Tell your mom I might eat dinner over at Sarah's house."

"What movie?" Tia asked. "I haven't been to a movie in weeks."

"Oh, just something light and stupid that you'd find boring," Tamera said. "I wouldn't want to keep you from your homework."

Then she danced out the front door. Tia swallowed hard, fighting back the tears. Until now Tamera would never have gone to a movie without her. And she'd never have hung out at Sarah's house without inviting her along, too. Obviously Tamera was embarrassed to be seen with her. She didn't want her around anymore.

The next day Tia was in the middle of math class when the door opened and a strange girl came in.

"Sorry to interrupt, Mrs. Heffernan," she said, "but is Tia Landry in here? She's wanted in the office right away."

"Oooh, Tia," Ronald Jones behind her teased. "What have you been doing now?"

"Tia's in trouble," Mark White said delightedly. "Tia, have you been cloning football players again?"

Tia could hear the chuckles around her. She shot Tamera a worried look as she got to her feet. Tamera shrugged.

"Run along, Tia," Mrs. Heffernan said kindly. "I don't think you'll be missing anything in the next few minutes. We'll only be going over what we learned about triangle proofs."

"And she knew it all the first time," someone behind Tia muttered.

"Don't be stupid. She wrote the book." Tia heard Ronald's voice answer.

She felt her cheeks burning as she hurried out of the classroom. What could they want with her in the office? The girl hadn't said the principal's office, had she? She was sure she hadn't done anything wrong, but the thought of going to the office always made her heart race. At least she knew there couldn't be any problem at home, or Tamera would have been called out of class, too.

She took a deep breath before she pushed open the office door. "Are you Tia?" the woman at the front desk asked her. "Go on through, dear. Mrs. Chang wanted to see you in the counselor's office."

The counselor's office, Tia told herself. That couldn't be too bad. In fact it might even be good. Maybe they wanted to tell her about science scholarships. She knocked and went in.

"Tia?" Mrs. Chang looked up from her desk. "Sit down, honey. I understand you've just been asked to join the Future Female Scientists. Congratulations. That's an honor for a sophomore, you know."

Tia smiled shyly.

"And they've submitted your name as a possible tutor in our student mentor program. Normally we don't include sophomores, but since you've been so highly recommended and we are in desperate need of more tutors this year, I thought I'd ask you. Would you be interested in becoming a tutor, Tia?"

"What does it involve?" Tia asked cautiously.

"You have to commit to at least an hour per week," Mrs. Chang said. "Any more than that can be arranged between you and the student you are helping. And you get paid, of course. The going rate is five dollars an hour. You'll hardly get rich but . . ."

"It's better than doing it for nothing," Tia said.

"And easier work than washing up at the Rocket Burger."

Mrs. Chang smiled. "It's not always so easy," she said. "Students like yourself sometimes find it hard to understand that other students don't find math and science easy. It can take a lot of patience."

"I'm good at explaining things," Tia said. "I've had to clue in my sister before now."

"Ah, yes. Tamera," Mrs. Chang said, nodding. "How's she doing? Any better?"

"Okay, I guess," Tia said.

"If only some of your work habits could rub off on her," Mrs. Chang said. "I'm sure she could be a good student like you."

"That's what her dad keeps telling her," Tia said. "But I don't think it does any good. I think it just annoys her."

"It would probably annoy me, too," Mrs. Chang said with a laugh. "So how about it, Tia? Can I sign you up as a tutor, or do you want to think about it first?"

"I'll think about it," Tia said. "I have to decide whether I have the time right now. The Einsteinettes have a lot of projects going. Heather Braunschweiger and I have volunteered to be mentors at the little kids' science fair. That's going to take time."

"I understand," Mrs. Chang said. "But it would be great if you could take on a tutoring assignment. We have a lot of students who need extra help right now. I'd hate to see some of them drop out because they can't keep up."

"I'll let you know soon, Mrs. Chang," Tia said. Mrs. Chang nodded. "Very good."

"What was that all about?" Tamera asked as Tia came back to the classroom just as the bell rang.

"Mrs. Chang asked me to be a peer tutor," Tia said.

"Great, you can start with me." Tamera grinned. "I couldn't understand a word of what Mrs. Heffernan was saying today."

"I have to charge you five dollars an hour," Tia said, grinning back at her sister.

"Don't I get a family discount rate?"

"Well, maybe four fifty, seeing that you're my twin."

"Thanks for nothing," Tamera quipped.

Tia laughed. It felt great to be kidding around with Tamera again. Maybe things were back to normal between them.

Tamera crammed the last of her books into her backpack and slung it over her shoulder. "On second thought I'd rather spend the money at the mall with Sarah this afternoon," she said.

"You're going to the mall with Sarah again?" Tia asked.

"Sure. Why not? You'll be saving the world with Heather; I'll be boosting the economy by shopping with Sarah," Tamera said smoothly. "See ya later."

Tia watched her sister go. The lump returned to her throat. She found herself wishing that she had never been elected to the stupid Einsteinettes. She had been so proud when they had chosen her. She had loved being the center of attention at home, seeing her mother and Ray so proud of her. She had loved being an instant celebrity at school. She had felt all warm and proud inside when even seniors came up to her or pointed her out to each other.

But now she wasn't so sure anymore. Had the kids at school only wanted to know who she was so that they could laugh at her behind her back? Did everyone secretly think she was a geek, like Tamera said? And, worst of all, had she lost her sister's friendship forever?

Chapter 8

❧❧

"Hey, Tia, guess what?" Tamera yelled as she burst in through the front door. "Sarah's parents say that she can have a girl-boy party for her birthday, so we have to find cute dates in a hurry—"

She stopped in her tracks as she saw Tia sitting on the sofa, with Roger beside her.

Roger looked up at her and beamed. "What a dilemma. Do I escort the crazy, fun sister or the serious, brainy sister? What a choice to have to make."

"I'll make it for you, Roger," Tamera said. "Neither sister. You're not invited." She looked across at Tia. "What's he doing here?" she demanded.

"Tia invited me over," Roger said smugly.

"Tia, I know this science thing has affected your

taste in clothes, but not your taste in boys, too?" Tamera said with a disgusted look on her face.

"I'm doing a behavioral science experiment," Tia said. "If it works on Roger, I'll know that the little kids can do it for their science fair."

"So you're sort of using Roger instead of a rat?" Tamera grinned. "That makes sense. Only rats are cuter. They have adorable little twitchy whiskers." She snatched up the pile of colored blocks that were in front of Roger on the coffee table. "Okay, Roger. Experiment over. Get lost."

"Tamera, don't speak to him like that," Tia said. "Roger is a fellow human being and should be treated with respect."

"Sorry," Tamera said. "Okay, Roger. *Please* get lost." She turned to Tia. "Better?"

Roger got to his feet. "It's pretty obvious that your sister doesn't have your brainpower, Tia," he said. "She hasn't learned the art of communication yet."

"Don't tempt me, Roger, or I'll be forced to communicate with you," Tamera said, waving a fist in his direction.

"Like I said, still at the caveman level," Roger commented to Tia as he moved away from Tamera. "Evolution hasn't reached her yet. I think I'd be safer going to the party with you, Tia. We could have long intellectual discussions while the rest of the kids waste their time dancing. What do you say?"

"I'll think about it," Tia said. " 'Bye now."

"You'll think about it?" Tamera demanded as Roger closed the door behind him. "Are you out of your mind, Tia. That was Roger. Roger the creepy little two-foot dwarf. You couldn't bring him to Sarah's party. There's no way they'd let you in."

"I didn't say I was going to bring him," Tia said. "It's just that Heather has made me more aware about respecting other people's feelings and rights." She got up and started clearing her papers from the table. "I don't know that I'd want to go to Sarah's party anyway, after the way you guys laughed at me. I wouldn't want to risk being laughed at again."

"Tia, of course you have to come to the party," Tamera said.

"They'd want the Queen of the Geeks there?" Tia snapped. "What for? Another good laugh?"

"Tia, what's happening to you?" Tamera said. "You've always loved parties as much as I have. And you know any party at Sarah's house will be fun. Her boyfriend, Adam, knows some cool guys so you don't even have to bring a date, if you can't find one. Just don't bring one of your Future Male Scientists, okay?"

"See what I mean?" Tia said. "You guys will only make fun of me."

"We won't," Tamera said. "And everyone will know you've definitely turned into a nerd if you don't come." She took off her backpack and dumped it on the sofa. "Now, if you'll excuse me, I've got to get busy." She took out her notebook and started scribbling in it.

"Tamera, I'm impressed," Tia said. "You're actually starting on your homework before you snack?"

"My homework?" Tamera laughed. "I'm making a list of all the guys I know. I'm determined to bring my own date to Sarah's party. Somehow I've got to come up with an available hunk in the next two weeks. I wonder what Clyde would say if I went up to him and introduced myself and invited him to the party."

"He'd laugh," Tia said. "Or he'd do what you did to Roger. He'd tell you to get lost."

"I don't see why," Tamera said. "I'm a fun person. And I'm creative, too. I'll come up with someone . . . and I'll need a killer new outfit. I'll have to start working on my dad."

"Working on your dad for what?" Ray asked, coming in from the kitchen with a cup of coffee in his hand.

"A new outfit for Sarah's party," Tamera said excitedly. "It's going to be a real grown-up boy-girl party with dancing and—"

"Oh, no," Ray said swiftly.

"What's wrong, Daddy?"

Ray was still shaking his head. "You're too young for that sort of thing."

"Daddy, I'm fifteen years old," Tamera said. "Besides, Tia will be there with me, won't you?" She looked across at Tia for support.

"I can't see Lisa letting her daughter go to that kind of party, either," Ray said.

"My mom knows that I'm a mature, responsible person," Tia said. "I'm sure she'd trust me to go to a party."

"She's in the kitchen. Why don't you ask her," Ray suggested with a grin.

"Okay, I will," Tia said. She pushed open the kitchen door. Lisa was at the table with dress patterns spread around her. She was muttering "Where is piece number four? There *has* to be a piece number four...."

She looked up as Tia stood in front of her. "There's no bodice," she said to Tia. "How can I make a dress with no bodice?"

"It has to be there," Tia said. "Mom, listen up. I want to ask you a question."

"Piece number four . . . What is it, honey?"

"You'd let me go to a party, wouldn't you?" Tia asked sweetly. "You'd trust me to behave."

"Sure," Lisa said. "Just as long as it's at some-one's house I know and it's over by ten and there are no boys there."

"Mom!" Tia wailed as Ray and Tamera gave each other a knowing look.

"You see, Lisa completely agrees with me," Ray said. "You're both too young for that kind of thing. Next year, maybe."

"Dad, come on, this is the twentieth century, not the Dark Ages," Tamera said.

"We'll talk about it later," Ray said. "Maybe Lisa and I can go visit Sarah's parents and volunteer to help chaperon the party."

"Chaperon?" Tamera wailed. "Dad, that would wreck our evening. Tia and I can chaperon each other."

"From what I've heard about Sarah, her parents allow her way too much freedom," Ray said.

"And they let her date that no-good guy Adam," Lisa added. "Remember when he came sneaking around here and climbed into your slumber party? I don't want my daughter involved in that kind of hanky-panky again."

"Lisa, that was only fun," Tamera said.

"And I'm more mature and sensible now, Mom," Tia added.

Lisa looked up thoughtfully, then nodded. "What am I thinking about? You're a future scientist now, aren't you? I don't know why you'd even want to go to a party like that, Tia honey. It sounds way below your intellectual level. You should be hanging out with smart people, going to lectures and museums. Which reminds me—I saw this ad on the bus today. I almost signed you up for your next summer vacation."

"A tour of Europe?" Tia asked.

"Computer camp," Lisa said.

"Computer camp?" Tia exclaimed. "Mom, have you seen the kind of kids who go to computer camp? They're all total nerds."

"I'll go get your pocket protector," Tamera said smugly.

That night Tia lay in bed, staring at the ceiling and listening to Tamera's steady breathing. She would have liked to talk to her sister, but Tamera wasn't on her side anymore.

What have I done? she asked herself. Everything Tamera had said was true. The whole world now thought of her as a geek. Who cared if she was the greatest scientific brain if everyone thought she was a weirdo? Tamera was right, she decided. High school wasn't just about studying. It was about having fun and making friends and trying lots of new things. She had to do something to save her image before it was too late.

The next morning she went straight into Mrs. Chang's office.

"I've been thinking about tutoring," she said, "and I've decided that it's not really something I want to do right now. I don't have the time."

"That's a pity, Tia," Mrs. Chang said, "because I think you'd be good at it. And I do have some students in urgent need of tutoring right now. You couldn't manage just one hour a week?"

"I don't think so," Tia said. She wanted to say that tutoring was one more thing that was bad for her image. Fun and cool kids didn't tutor. They were out hanging together at the mall.

"Okay, I understand," Mrs. Chang said. "You

young people are all horribly overscheduled. Maybe later you'll reconsider if you have more time."

She looked up as there was a tap on her door. Mr. Washington, another counselor, came in. "Another student request for tutoring," he said. "They keep on coming." He looked at Tia. "Did you manage to recruit this young lady? We're especially short of math tutors."

"She's too busy, unfortunately," Mrs. Chang said. She opened the book in front of her. "So this is another request for a math tutor, is it? What's the name?"

"Hemming," Mr. Washington said. "Clyde Hemming."

Tia didn't think she had heard right. "Clyde Hemming?" she asked. It came out as a squeak.

"Yes, do you know him?" Mr. Washington said. "I believe he's also a sophomore. I understand he's having severe problems with geometry and he might have to drop the class."

"I'll do it," Tia blurted out. "I changed my mind. I have enough time, after all. And I should be helping my fellow students so that they don't have to drop classes, shouldn't I?"

"Why, thank you, Tia," Mrs. Chang said. "That's very public spirited of you. I'm sure Clyde will be very grateful."

Tia couldn't wait to get out of Mrs. Chang's office. She sprinted down the halls, mowing down students as she passed. She just had to find Tamera before she went to her first class.

Tamera was just closing her locker.

"Tamera, wait up!" Tia yelled. "You'll never guess in a million years what's happened now."

"What can it be this time? Future lawyers club? Future doctors club?"

A big, smug smile spread across Tia's face. "I've been asked to tutor Clyde Hemming in math," she said.

Tamera's mouth dropped open. "*The* Clyde Hemming? The hunk? The babe? The drop-dead gorgeous Clyde Hemming?"

"How many sophomores called Clyde Hemming can there be?"

"You're joking, right?" Tamera asked.

"I'm telling the truth, Tamera." Tia beamed. "I just came from Mrs. Chang's office. See what I've got here? It's Clyde's home number. I've got to call him at home tonight."

Tamera threw her arms up in the air. "Yesss!" she yelled. "It's finally happening. I knew it would, sooner or later. Tia, you're incredible. I'm sorry I ever called you a geek."

Tia smiled at her sister, before Tamera went on. "You're actually going to be tutoring the guy of my dreams. I'm finally going to meet Clyde Hemming!"

"Maybe, sometime," Tia said cautiously.

"What do you mean, 'maybe, sometime'?"

"I'll have to see how it goes first, Tamera."

"It's simple, Tia. We can find a way to sneak me in with you. Hey, I've got an idea—you need an assistant, right? How about if I come along to carry your books for you?"

"No, Tamera."

"Or I could bring a blackboard to write the problems on. I've got very neat printing."

"No, Tamera."

"Or I could carry a fan for you, in case it got too hot in there, or an umbrella in case you had to walk home in the rain. . . ."

"Tamera, forget it. You're not coming with me when I go to tutor Clyde."

"Why not?" Tamera asked, pouting.

"Because I'm being paid to tutor Clyde, not sneak strange girls into his house."

"In that case, when there's a break in the math, don't forget to ask him if he'd be my date for Sarah's party."

"Tamera!" Tia laughed. "I don't even know the guy yet. I can't just come out and ask him personal stuff."

"Sure you can, favorite sister in the world," Tamera said, throwing her arms around Tia. "It will be a piece of cake. Think of it—you'll be sitting there alone in Clyde's room, your heads close together as you study the book. Maybe your hands will brush as you turn the pages. Maybe his leg will touch yours. You look up, and your eyes meet, and you say to him, 'I have a sister who has a crush on you and would like to ask you to a party. She's like me, only cuter.' "

"Tamera!" Tia exploded, pushing her sister away. "You really are something else. If I was getting along that well with him, maybe I'd want to ask him to the party myself."

"But you don't have a mega crush on him like I do," Tamera wailed. "And he's not your type. You need someone smart and scientific."

"You told me last night that I'd better not bring any future scientists to Sarah's party. I don't think any of your friends would laugh if I brought Clyde."

"Tia, you wouldn't." Tamera signed. "Not after I've dreamed of dating Clyde for so long. Not after I've tried my hardest to come up with ways to meet him. You couldn't be so mean as to take him for yourself."

"Hey, you know what they say," Tia said. "All's fair in love and war."

"If you're thinking of going after Clyde Hemming, then this *is* going to be war, sister," Tamera said. "Because I'm going to come up with a way to meet him somehow. And when he sees you and me together and he notices my sparkling personality and how fine I'm looking, there will be no contest, sis. He'll have to like me better."

"Well see about that," Tia said. Finally she had a chance to show Tamera who was the geek. Just wait until Sarah and Michelle and the others saw her with Clyde Hemming. Then they wouldn't be laughing anymore. They'd be crying with envy.

Chapter 9

∞∞

Tia went through the day with a big smile on her face. She couldn't believe her luck. First the Einstein-ettes, and now this. Principal Vernon was right—hard work really did pay off. If she hadn't been such a good student, she'd never have gotten to tutor Clyde.

It was amazing how one little thing could change her life, she decided. All those people who teased her for being a geek now acted as if she was Ms. Cool. Tamera must have told all her friends, because they crowded around her the second she came into the cafeteria at lunchtime.

"Is it really true? You're going to be tutoring Clyde Hemming?" Michelle asked.

"I am so jealous!" Sarah said. "Some people have all the luck."

"Sarah, you've got a great boyfriend," Francine said. "Why should you be jealous? Think of us who don't have dates for your party yet."

"We can't all share Clyde," Chantal said bluntly. "And if Tia's smart, she'll snag him for herself."

"If Tia plays her cards right, maybe she can find dates for all of us," Michelle said. "Clyde has a whole bunch of cute friends. And I know Tia won't forget about her old buddies, right, Tia?"

"I'm only tutoring him, Michelle," Tia said. "I'm not setting up a dating service with him." She wanted to remind them that they had laughed at her and called her Queen of the Geeks only a couple of days ago, but she was enjoying being in the center of things again.

"It's simple, Tia," Chantal said. "You help him with his math and earn his undying gratitude. You two become best buddies. You get invited to his famous parties, and then you mention casually that you have these cute, adorable friends who'd just love to come to the next party with you."

"I'll do what I can," Tia said, "but I'm not promising anything."

"I think your friend's trying to get your attention," Chantal said with a grin.

Tia looked up to see Heather waving at her from the cafeteria doorway. Tia went across to her. "Come and join us. We're just about to have lunch," she said.

"I don't have time to eat," Heather said. "I

wanted to check on something I saw on the news last night. I thought you might want to come to the library with me."

"I'm kind of hungry," Tia said. "I'll come and join you when I've finished eating."

"Okay," Heather said. She looked annoyed. "You're eating with those girls?"

"They're my friends."

"Really? They didn't look too friendly last time we saw them."

"They were just kidding around," Tia said. "They're great kidders."

"Oh, and I meant to tell you. It's definitely okay for Friday night. I asked my Dad."

"Friday night?" For a second Tia drew a blank.

"You remember, I told you that my dad was taking me to a lecture at Wayne State about the latest discoveries on Jupiter?"

"Oh, right," Tia said.

"And you said you'd like to come, too," Heather reminded her. "So I asked my dad, and he said it was fine with him. And my mom said you could sleep over afterward."

"Cool," Tia said. "Thanks, Heather."

She was glad that Michelle and the others were far enough away not to hear. She knew they'd think that a lecture about a planet was a really dorky way to spend an evening. But the way Heather had talked about it had made it sound exciting. Now she wasn't sure that she wanted to go anymore, but she couldn't say no without hurting Heather's feelings.

"It's going to be fun," Heather said. "We'll have so much to talk about, I'll bet we don't sleep at all."

Tia smiled, then she remembered her really big news. "Guess what, Heather. I just got my first tutoring assignment."

"You did?"

"Yeah, and I'm so excited. I'm going to be tutoring Clyde Hemming."

"Why are you excited about that?" Heather asked with a puzzled look. "I shouldn't think that tutoring him would be very intellectually challenging."

It was Tia's turn to look puzzled. "Clyde Hemming? You know, the cute guy who drives the black Camaro?"

"Rather you than me," Heather said. She looked as if there were a bad smell under her nose. "He's in one of my classes. He's a total goof-off. Either that or he's unintelligent. I think you've got a tough assignment."

"Tough assignment—in the same room as Clyde Hemming?" Tia exclaimed.

"Don't tell me you find that kind of guy attractive?"

"Sure. Doesn't everyone? He's a hunk, Heather."

"He's not my type. I go for brains rather than brawn," Heather said. "But if you're looking forward to meeting him, then good luck, I guess. I hope it turns out well for you."

*   *   *

Tia thought about this conversation as she sat on the bus going home from school. Heather might be smart, but sometimes she was also totally clueless, she decided. When it came to boys, Heather was from another planet. Where do I belong? she wondered. I just want to be an ordinary teenager. I want to do well at school, but I want to like the things other people like and have fun, too. And I do want a boyfriend some time soon.

"Well, go on, call him," Tamera commanded the moment Tia came through the front door. She rushed ahead and snatched up the phone, holding it out for Tia to take.

"Chill out, Tamera. He's probably not even home yet. Guys like Clyde don't rush straight home from school. They hang with friends."

"What are you going to say to him?" Tamera asked.

"What do you mean? I'm going to say 'Hi, I'm your new tutor. When would you like me to work with you?' "

"Is that all? That sounds like a boring person."

"So what would you say?"

"I'd say, in my most sexy voice, 'Hi there. I'm Tia. I want to teach you that one plus one makes a couple. How about a date?' "

Tia started laughing. "You know you'd never say that."

Tamera was laughing, too. "I know, but you

should try to sound like someone fun, or he'll get the wrong impression."

"Thanks for the advice, but I'd rather sound like me."

"Don't forget you've got that geeky image to live down. You don't want Clyde to think of you as his boring Einsteinette tutor, do you? They say first impressions stick." Another thought struck her. "And what are you going to wear? You can't look like a Heather clone or he'll never let you in the door." She grabbed Tia's arm. "Come upstairs. We'd better start going through your wardrobe and throwing away all those disgusting outfits. From now on you have to start looking good! You can borrow my black tank top if you like, and those black jeans—they're totally cool. They'll look great on you."

"Tamera, hold on a second," Tia said, shaking her sister loose. "Will you stop trying to run my life for me?"

"But you're my sister. Dorkiness rubs off, you know. If Clyde thinks you're a dork, he might think I'm one, too."

"Since you're not going to be meeting him, I guess that doesn't matter."

"Don't be so sure about that," Tamera said. "I've got plans."

"I'm warning you, Tamera. You'd better not try butting in on my tutoring, or I'll tell your dad."

"Tattletale," Tamera snapped. Then she paused

and said in a softer voice, "Come on, Tia. You don't really want him for yourself, do you? You said yourself that you'd want a serious, scientific kind of guy."

"And you told me that everyone would laugh at me if I brought that kind of guy to the party, remember? Maybe I don't enjoy being laughed at."

"I was only teasing, Tia. I didn't mean it. I don't really think you're geeky."

"You won't think I'm geeky when I'm invited to Clyde's next party," Tia said smoothly. "Now, if you'll excuse me, I'm going to make a phone call."

An hour later Tia was on her way to Clyde's house. She couldn't believe how smoothly the call had gone. She had told Clyde she was his tutor, and he'd asked if she could come over right away. He'd even offered to come and pick her up in his car. But it turned out he lived only a few blocks away, and Tia had offered to walk.

She had refused Tamera's offer of the black jeans, but she had changed into her favorite blue jeans and her new Harvard sweatshirt.

I hope I don't clam up when I meet him, she thought. I hope I can remember how to do math when he's sitting close to me. Then she stopped herself. Wait a second—this was all an act, wasn't it? She knew that Tamera really had a big crush on Clyde, but she didn't, too, did she? She agreed that he was drop-dead cute and that he was the guy any sophomore girl would have killed to date. But did she really want him for herself? Wasn't that just something she had said to get back at Tamera? If she did manage to get a date with Clyde, wouldn't it just be to show Tamera once and for all that she was not a geek.

As Tia got closer and closer to Clyde's house, she wasn't sure anymore. Her heart was beating very fast, and she was finding it hard to breathe. Just don't let me look like an idiot when I meet him, she prayed.

She started rehearsing what she was going to say, in case Clyde's mother opened the doorb. But it was Clyde himself.

"Hi," he said. "Are you Tia, the math whiz? Boy, you don't know how glad I am to see you." He gave her the most wonderful smile. "Come on in." He held open the door for her.

He was even cuter close up, Tia decided. She glanced back at the street, half hoping that someone from school would be passing and see her going into Clyde's house. But the street was empty.

Clyde led the way into the living room. There were math books and papers on the coffee table.

"I have to get the hang of math in a hurry," he said over his shoulder to her. "My dad's threatened to take away my car if I flunk math. And I'm just about to flunk it."

"I'm sure I can help you," Tia said. "I'm good at explaining things."

Clyde turned to face her and smiled again. "I'm counting on you, Tia," he said. His whole face lit up when he smiled, she noticed. And his eyelashes were unfairly long for a guy.

Stay calm, Tia, she told herself.

Clyde flopped onto the sofa and held up a sheet of paper. "Homework tonight. Twenty problems and I don't get any of them," he said. He tossed her the paper as she sat down cautiously at the edge of the sofa.

Tia glanced over the paper. "These aren't hard," she said. "They're all proofs about parallel lines and triangles."

"Great." Clyde beamed at her. "So we can get through them in a hurry, right? I told my buddies I'd meet them at six."

"Maybe we should look at why you don't understand them, Clyde," Tia said. "It would make more sense to start at the beginning."

"I don't have time for that," he said. "In fact I was kind of hoping you'd do me a favor."

"And?" she asked cautiously.

"And do these for me."

"You want me to do your homework for you? Clyde, that's not what I'm here for. I'm supposed to tutor you so that you understand, not do your work for you."

"Hey, what does it matter who does the work as long as I pass the class?"

"It will matter to you when you find yourself

flunking next year because you didn't understand this year's concepts."

Clyde was looking at her with those smoldering dark eyes. "You're right, Tia," he said, "but I thought, maybe just this once you could help me out. You see, I promised the guys, and they'll be waiting for me. If you could just zip through these problems for me tonight, I swear I'll try and understand next time. You could come over tomorrow. We could work every afternoon this week."

"But, Clyde . . ." Tia could feel herself weakening. She knew she should be strong and refuse to do his work, but the problem was that she was finding it hard to say no to him. If she didn't help him out this time, he could easily ask for another tutor and she'd be back to being Tia the geek.

"Please, Tia," he whispered. "Pretty please with sugar on top?"

Tia had to laugh. Clyde was laughing, too.

"You're terrible," she said.

"That's what all the girls say," he said. "But I'm fun, right? I'm not boring."

"No, you're definitely not boring," she said.

"And adorable, too?" he teased. "All the girls say I'm adorable."

"Huh," Tia said, fighting to stay cool. "Let's get to work and see if you can do any of these problems."

"I like you, Tia," Clyde said. "You're different from the other girls. Do you know how many girls at our school would kill to be sitting here beside me? Do you know how many girls would pay to do my home-work? But you're strong. I like strong women."

Tia suddenly realized that she wanted to laugh. Clyde might be cute, but he had an ego the size of Texas!

"So tell me all about it!" Tamera yelled, grabbing Tia as she came into the house. "Every single detail. Did you sit together on the sofa? Did your hands brush as you turned over the page? Did he look at you with those dark, flashing eyes?"

Tia wanted to tell her sister that Clyde's ego had completely turned her off. Even if he was the most gorgeous guy in the state of Michigan, she wouldn't want to go out with him. But she had to get even with Tamera. She had to pay her back for all those put-downs.

She gave her sister a big, smug smile. "All of the above and more," she said.

Chapter 10

෧෧

$\mathcal{T}$amera was feeling very low. Nothing was working out the way she wanted. She and Tia had gotten along so well since they'd met. She had loved having her twin around. They'd had such fun together until this dumb science club thing.

Since then everything had gone wrong. She had been jealous of all the fuss everyone made of Tia when she joined the science club. She had felt small and stupid and not good at anything. So she had started teasing Tia, and the teasing had really worked. Tia didn't enjoy being labeled a geek. But Tamera hadn't expected in a million years that Tia would switch from geek to Ms. Popularity in one week!

Tia hadn't said much about what happened at

Clyde's house, but it was pretty obvious that she and Clyde had gotten along really well. And she had gone back the next day and the next, too. Tamera had kept telling herself that Clyde must think of Tia as a brain, not a person. But then yesterday he had actually come up to her in the cafeteria.

"Hey there, miracle worker. I got a B plus on my homework assignment, thanks to you," he said, putting his hand on Tia's shoulder. Then he looked at the surprised faces of the other girls at the table. "Do you know who this girl really is?" he asked them. "She's my guardian angel. She's taking good care of me, right, Tia?" And he stood there, looking down at Tia with those dark, gorgeous eyes.

Tamera had thought she'd explode with jealousy, right there on the spot. But she'd managed to keep her face calm until Clyde ruffled Tia's hair and said, "See ya tonight then?" and walked away.

When lunch was over, Tamera and Sarah walked to class together.

"How about that, Clyde and Tia?" Sarah asked, a big grin spreading across her face. "Who would have thought it?"

"She's just his math tutor, Sarah," Tamera said coldly. "He was just grateful that she's helping him."

"You think that's all it was?" Sarah asked. "They sure looked kind of friendly to me. Amazing. I'd have thought Tia was the last girl that Clyde would have looked at."

"He wasn't looking at her, except to tell her she

was a great tutor," Tamera snapped, feeling definitely angry now. "How could Clyde possibly be interested in Tia? I mean, what could they have to talk about—he'd be talking fast cars and parties when she'd be talking molecules and ozone layers."

Sarah shrugged. "I guess you're right. I hope she hasn't forgotten about getting you guys dates for my party. You'd better remind her."

"Don't worry," Tamera said. "I will." As she left Sarah, worry lines wrinkled her forehead. It couldn't be true that Clyde really liked Tia, could it?

Get real, Tamera told herself. Clyde and Tia? Give me a break! But then she remembered the way he had stood there with his hand on Tia's shoulder. Was that how you treated your tutor? No way! she wanted to yell. Tia just isn't his type. What he needs is someone cute and fun-loving like me. I know he'd like me better if he got a chance to meet me. But that was never going to happen if Tia kept him to herself.

Then Tamera remembered what her father had said to her when she was little: "Tamera, you can't just sit back and let things happen. Sometimes you've got to make them happen, if you want them badly enough."

And I do want this, real bad, she told herself.

That afternoon Tamera put on her wildest, coolest outfit—her black velvet jacket, white lace blouse, the tight black jeans, and the floppy black velvet hat with the big red rose at the front, and was about to tiptoe out the front door when Lisa came in.

"My, aren't you looking good!" she exclaimed. "Where are you off to?"

"Just going over to a friend's house to hang out," Tamera said, knowing that Tia was sitting in the living room and would hear every word.

"I don't believe it for a second." Lisa laughed. "Nobody gets dressed up like that for a girlfriend. You must have a secret motive."

"We might go down to the mall later," Tamera said. "And we might meet these guys again, so I want to look good."

Lisa raised her eyes. "You'd better not let your daddy know that you're sneaking out to meet guys," she said. "He'll have you locked away in a convent until you turn thirty-five."

"Lisa, this is totally harmless. We're only going to talk to them at the mall. What could happen?"

"Every big thing starts little," Lisa said, "and I know how your daddy feels. He wants to stop you girls from growing up too fast, just like I do. I don't want to let my baby out of my sight until she turns twenty-one. No, make that thirty-five, too." She wagged a warning finger at Tamera. "So make sure you're back here when your daddy gets home, if you're smart."

"Don't worry, I will," Tamera said. "Just don't mention this, okay, Lisa?"

Lisa put her finger to her mouth. "My lips are sealed, honey, just as long as you behave yourself."

Tamera blew a sigh of relief as Lisa finally shut the door. Then she sprinted down the street. That conversation had taken up too much of her precious time. Now she'd have to work very fast if she wanted to impress Clyde before Tia got there.

It was only when she knocked on Clyde's front door that her confidence left her. Did she have the nerve to go through with this? Tia would probably kill her and tell her father, and she'd get grounded for life. But if she finally got to speak to Clyde, it would be worth it. She had ten minutes at the most to convince him that she was the girl of his dreams, not Tia.

"Hi, I'm Tia's sister, Tamera," she rehearsed, practicing her most perky voice and winning smile. "Tia asked me to tell you she's running a little late."

The door opened.

Tamera froze. Clyde was actually standing there, two feet away from her, and he was smiling at her. She hadn't been prepared for how cute he was close up. She felt her legs turning to jelly. She opened her mouth but no sound came out. "Hi," she finally managed to squeak.

"You're early," Clyde said. "I wasn't expecting you for another ten minutes. Just give me a second to finish this sandwich."

He didn't wait for Tamera to say anything more

but headed for the kitchen, then reappeared with a monster sandwich that had to be six inches thick.

"Baloney and tuna fish and turkey breast and Swiss cheese," he mumbled with his mouth full. "I cleaned out the refrigerator. You want some?"

"Uh ... no, thanks," Tamera stammered.

"Okay, let's get started. I think I got the hang of most of that stuff you showed me," he went on. He flopped onto the sofa and patted the seat beside him. "Come on, don't just stand there. I've got a test tomorrow, and I'd like to ace it."

Tamera fought to make her vocal cords obey her. "Clyde, there's something I ought to tell you," she began, but the words came out barely louder than a mouse's squeak, and he was already flicking through the pages.

"Ah, here we are. Take a look at number three. I thought I'd got it, but the answer isn't right. So where did I go wrong, huh?" He thrust the notebook into her hands.

Tamera wasn't the world's best geometry student. She looked at the jumble of numbers. They all swam together. She felt as if every scrap of geometry she'd ever learned had been sucked from her brain.

"It looks fine to me," she muttered.

"But it isn't fine!" Clyde yelled. "I checked on the answer from this computer guy in my class, and he's got something totally different."

Tamera went on staring, trying desperately to

think of how to talk her way out of this without looking like an idiot.

"What was that theorem about parallelograms again?" Clyde went on. "You know what you told me yesterday about opposite angles are . . . what?"

"Across from each other?" Tamera suggested, wishing the ground would miraculously swallow her up. Why had she ever thought this was a good idea? Any second now she'd have to tell him she wasn't Tia, and he'd think she was the world's biggest weirdo. And she'd never have another chance with him, ever.

Clyde was looking at her strangely. "But you told me all about it yesterday. You said I'd never have problems if I remembered. Don't tell me you've forgotten now?"

Tamera took a really deep breath. "Look, Clyde, there's something you should know," she said. "You see, I'm not really . . . what I mean is, that I know you think that I'm—"

"Tamera?" a voice shrieked. "What are *you* doing here?"

Tia's face appeared at the open window. "I thought I heard your voice as I walked past the window, but I thought, no, that couldn't be my sister. She'd never do anything as sneaky as that. But I was wrong, wasn't I?"

"Tia?" Clyde asked cautiously. "Is that you?"

"You bet it is."

"Then who have I been talking to?"

"My twin sister, Tamera," Tia said. "I don't know what she thinks she's doing here."

"I came over to tell Clyde that you might be a little late," Tamera said.

"But I wasn't late. I had no intention of being late."

"So I was wrong," Tamera said with what she hoped was a winning smile. "You looked like you were running late to me, so I thought I'd do you a good turn and stop over on my way, just in case Clyde was wondering where you were. Just trying to help out, smooth things over so that he wasn't mad at you."

"I know why you're here, Tamera. I'm not stupid."

"So this is your sister," Clyde said with a big grin on his face.

"Yes, and she's just leaving," Tia said firmly. "Aren't you, Tamera?"

"Okay, okay," Tamera said. "Nice meeting you, Clyde. Just trying to help out, you know. Gotta run. 'Bye." She went on babbling and smiling like an idiot as she backed toward the front door, opened it, and fled. Now she had blown it forever with him.

"Sorry about that, Clyde," Tia said as she closed the door on her sister. "She makes me so mad."

"What's the problem?"

"She didn't come here to tell you I was running late. She came over here because she has a monster crush on you and she'd do anything to get to meet you."

"I can dig that," Clyde said smoothly. "Believe me, a lot of girls have tried to get into this house to meet me. I'm used to it." He paused and smiled at Tia. "That's why I like working with you, Tia. You're not one of those goofy girls. You're all business when you're here. I don't have to worry about fighting you off."

"You have to fight girls off?"

"All the time," he said, laughing. "Those girls are violent, you know. I've had to take karate lessons, just to be able to defend myself."

Tia laughed. "Clyde, you're so funny," she said. She snuck a look at him as he sat beside her on the sofa. Was it good or bad that he'd said that she wasn't like other girls? He'd said he like being around her, and that was good. But maybe he thought she was such a dork that he didn't have to think of her as a girl—and that wasn't so good.

I wouldn't be interested in him, anyway, she reminded herself. *He's conceited and he doesn't take anything seriously.*

"We're wasting valuable time. Let's get down to work, okay?" she said.

"Good idea. I've also got a history paper to write," Clyde said. "You don't happen to be a whiz at history, too, do you? You wouldn't like to earn a little extra money writing a history paper for me this evening?"

"Clyde, I keep on telling you that it doesn't help you when I do the work for you," Tia said.

"Sure it helps me," Clyde insisted. "It lets me have a life. And who needs to know history? When I graduate, nobody is going to ask me about Julius Caesar ever again."

"I'll help you with the paper if you like," Tia said, "but it has to be your own words."

"You dictate and I'll write." He grinned.

"Clyde! You're terrible!" She reached out and slapped his hand, then remembered who she was hitting and took her hand away hastily. "Okay, parallelograms," she said. "I think we'll have this nailed if we meet once more this week."

"Oh, I meant to tell you," Clyde said. "I'm not going to have any time on Friday. I've got to get ready for a party Friday night. My mom makes me move all the furniture into the garage, so we don't wreck it."

"You're having a party Friday night?"

"Uh-huh. One of my famous parties—I guess you've heard about them, huh?" he said.

"Who hasn't?" Tia said.

"You can come if you like," Clyde said.

"Me? You're inviting me to a party?"

"Sure, why not?"

"You don't really want me there." Tia could hardly get the words out. Half an hour ago she would have said that Clyde was a guy with a big ego, too cute for his own good. But now that he was looking at her, his eyes flirting with her, all she could think of was that she was sitting beside Clyde Hemming and he was inviting her to a party.

"I wouldn't have asked you if I didn't want you there," he said smoothly. "My parties are very select, you know."

"But—but I don't know any of your friends," Tia stammered. "I don't know if I'd fit in."

"Don't worry. I'll take care of you," he said. "Come. You'll have fun, I promise. We'll have a blast." He was smiling at her as he rested his hand on her knee, giving it a friendly squeeze.

"Okay, I will. Thanks, Clyde," Tia mumbled.

Her heart was beating so fast, she was finding it hard to breathe. The words rang in her head: Clyde Hemming has invited *me* to a party. She couldn't wait to get home and tell Tamera.

"Now, about that history paper . . ." Clyde said.

Chapter 11

❀

Tamera was already home and changed out of her killer outfit as Tia came in the door. Tamera jumped up guiltily from the sofa. "Look, I'm sorry, it was a dumb idea," she said. "He must think I'm a total freak now, right?"

"He says he's used to it. Girls fight over him all the time."

"Did he say he thought I was cute?"

"Tamera! We didn't discuss you after you left," Tia said. "But I guess he must think you look cute . . ."

"Are you serious?"

"Because you look like me, and he thinks I'm cute enough to invite to his next party."

"His next party?" Tamera shrieked. "You've been invited to one of Clyde Hemming's parties?"

Tia clamped her hand swiftly over Tamera's mouth. "Shhh. Do you want my mother to hear?"

"You're right," Tamera said in a low voice. "She'd never let you go in a million years."

"We can't talk about it here," Tia muttered. She grabbed her sister and dragged her up the stairs to their room. "I have to go to that party, Tamera," she said as soon as she had safely shut the door. "There's no way I could not go to Clyde's party. You've got to help me."

"Let me get this straight," Tamera said. "You want me to help *you* get together with the guy of *my* dreams?"

"It will be good for you, too," Tia said.

"Run that by me again?"

"Don't you see?" Tia explained patiently. "If I got to Clyde's party, then I'm in with his friends, right? My reputation is made around school. I'd be Tia, the cool kid who hangs with Clyde."

"Yeah, but how does that help me?"

"Then the next time they do something fun, I can ask to bring my sister along. You'll get to meet his friends. You'll get to know him. You will also be known as super-cool around school."

Tamera nodded. "That's true, I guess," she said at last. Then she sighed and sank onto her bed. "But it's no good talking about it, because your mother is never going to let you go."

"I know that," Tia said. "If she freaked out about

Sarah's party, there's no way she'd ever say yes to Clyde's. What am I going to do, Tamera?"

"You're the one with the brains. Think of something."

"Yeah, but you're the one with the cunning. You've talked your way out of lots more trouble than I have. You've sneaked behind your dad's back enough times. You should be an expert at this."

"It shouldn't be too hard," Tamera said. "All you need is to invent some kind of dorky thing you'd do with your Einstein friends. Your mom would never say no to that—a visit to the museum or a lecture or—"

"Oh, no!" Tia let out a huge wail. "I've just remembered. I can't go to Clyde's party on Friday night—I really do have a dorky thing to do."

She flung herself back onto her bed. "I've blown it, Tamera. I've blown my one chance with Clyde!"

Tamera sat up cautiously. "What dorky thing?"

Tia sighed. "I promised Heather I'd go with her to a lecture about Jupiter."

Tamera let out a big splutter of laughter. "Yeah, that would be a tough choice. Should I go to a lecture about the planet Jupiter or to Clyde Hemming's party? Hard to decide which would be more fun."

"Of course I want to go to Clyde's party, but I've already said yes to Heather."

"No big deal. Tell her about Clyde's party. She'll understand."

"No, she won't," Tia said. "She thinks Clyde is one stage above pond scum. She despises him."

"Boy, she's even weirder than I thought," Tamera said. "Okay, so just tell her something else has come up and you'll do Jupiter another time."

"I can't do that. She was really looking forward to it. She has it all arranged with her parents for me to sleep over after the lecture."

"So?" Tamera demanded. "You're telling me that you're not going to Clyde's party because you've got to go to a lecture with Heather?"

"I can't let her down, Tamera."

"Think of a creative excuse, for pete's sake. Use that giant brain of yours. Tell her the satellite is still processing the latest information on Jupiter and you want to wait until it's all in." She went over to Tia and grabbed her. "This is Clyde Hemming, Tia. This is the one chance in your life to get in with the in crowd. Hang out with Clyde's crowd and you're made for life. And it won't hurt me, either, because I hang where you hang."

"But I can't let Heather down, even if I could sneak past my mom." Tia jumped up suddenly and started pacing the room. "I think I'm getting a brilliant idea, Tamera. I think I've found a way to go to Clyde's party and not disappoint Heather."

"Take Heather with you? Boy, that should be a real crowd pleaser. I just hope they're not serving hamburgers!"

"Listen up a second!" Tia yelled, dancing excitedly now. "This should work perfectly. We ask our parents if we can both sleep over at Heather's."

"Excuse me? You want me to hang out with a geek?"

"Shut up, please. This is important. We tell Heather that our parents are going to be out late and you get scared in the house alone, so we ask her if you can sleep over as well, after we come back from the lecture."

"I don't see how this is going to get you to Clyde's party," Tamera interrupted.

Tia waved her arms excitedly. "We say we're both going to sleep over at Heather's house. Then I go to Clyde's party instead, and you show up at Heather's dressed as me. You go to the lecture, I go to the party, and then I come back to Heather's house after you get back from the lecture. We spend the night at Heather's, and nobody is any the wiser. Brilliant, huh?"

"Except for one small thing."

"What?"

"That you imagine I'd spend an entire evening with Heather, pretending to be you, and she won't know the difference."

"It will be easy," Tia said. "You'll be at a lecture most of the time until I show up. You won't have to say a word or do a thing. Anyway, you can pull it off if anyone can, Tamera. I have great faith in your acting abilities."

"I know I could pull it off," Tamera said cautiously. "The question is, could I stand to be around Heather for that long? Do you think geekiness rubs off?"

"Tamera, I'd do the same for you, if you had the chance of a lifetime and you didn't want to blow it. We're sisters. We have to make sacrifices for each other."

"You can say that again," Tamera said. "Spending the entire evening alone with Heather, at a lecture on some old planet, knowing that you're with the guy of my dreams . . ." She picked up a white towel she had dropped on her chair and draped it around her head like a veil.

"What are you doing?" Tia asked.

"Practicing for when I'm made a saint," Tamera said. "Do you think there's already a Saint Tamera?"

"Shut up." Tia laughed, throwing her pillow at her sister.

Tamera suddenly pulled the towel off her head and threw it across to her sister. "Here, you need this more than me," she said. "You'd better start practicing now. And brush up on your chanting, too."

"What are you talking about?" Tia demanded, not knowing whether to laugh or not.

"Because if your mother finds out about this, you'll be heading straight for the nearest convent," Tamera said. "One with a ten-foot wall around it."

"She's not going to find out," Tia said confidently. "How could she find out? What could go wrong?"

"Oh, nothing," Tamera said breezily. "Only little things like Heather knowing I'm not you, or Heather's parents calling our parents, or someone seeing you going into Clyde's house."

"So you're saying you don't want to go through with this?" Tia asked.

"Oh, no, I said I'd do it," Tamera said. "It's no skin off my nose. If we get caught I'll say it was all your idea and you forced me to do it."

"Thanks a lot!" Tia said.

Tamera shrugged. "No sense in two of us being grounded until we're too old to date."

"You're worrying about nothing," Tia said. "My great brain will plan out all the details so there is no room for failure. And by Friday night it will be just me, Clyde, and my date with destiny!"

But on Friday evening, as Tia got ready for the party, inside the locked bathroom, she wasn't feeling quite so sure of herself. She was beginning to think that Tamera was right—if she got caught, she would be in major trouble. She'd probably also get her sister in major trouble.

She looked up and caught a glimpse of herself in the mirror. A strange, grown-up Tia looked back at her. She was wearing Tamera's shiny black tank top and tight black jeans. She had a big red flower pinned to her belt. Her hair was styled into a curly black mane around her head. Clyde would definitely think she looked good!

If my mom could see me now, she'd freak out, Tia thought, and immediately the guilt feelings she had tried to deny came flooding into her head. Her mom had been so great all these years, raising her alone to know right from wrong, going without so that Tia could always have the best. How can I let her down? she asked herself. She trusts me and I'm sneaking behind her back.

Then she stopped herself. Wait a second—she doesn't really trust me. She didn't even want me to go to Sarah's party, which was going to be totally tame. So tonight is just showing her that I am a mature person who can handle anything!

After that she felt a lot better. She pulled on her Harvard sweatshirt to hide the tank top and stuffed her makeup box into the overnight bag.

"Come on, Tia, we're going to be late," Tamera called. "You know the lecture starts at eight." She was wearing her black velvet jacket, so that she and Tia could trade clothes later.

Ray was sitting on the sofa, reading his paper, while Lisa was at the kitchen table, her mouth full of pins as she wrestled with yet another bridesmaid dress.

"That's a first for this house," Ray commented. "Tamera ready and on time, telling Tia to hurry up for a lecture. Maybe my little talks are rubbing off after all."

Lisa took the pins out of her mouth. "I think it's really sweet of Heather's parents to invite both girls," she said. "Heather must have known that Tamera would feel left out if only Tia slept over. I should call them and thank them."

The girls froze in horror on the stairs.

"It's okay, Mom. You don't have to call them," Tia said quickly. "They . . . they have this thing about not using the phone to save energy."

Lisa chuckled. "They sure are an interesting family. I wonder if you'll sleep with no covers tonight to save all those little ducks who make the comforters?"

"We're going now," Tia said. "See you guys in the morning."

Ray got to his feet.

"Where are you going, Dad?" Tamera asked nervously.

"I'm going to drive you over to Heather's house."

"That's okay," Tia said hastily. "We can walk. It's only a couple of blocks, and this is a very safe neighborhood, as you've said yourself."

"It's no problem," Ray said. "You've got bags to carry."

"But we like walking," Tia insisted. "It's good aerobic exercise, especially when we're carrying bags. And it's a lovely night. Perfect for walking."

Ray sat down again. "Okay, if that's what you really want."

"Those girls better not have anything sneaky

planned," Lisa called form the kitchen. "They'd better not be planning to meet any boys on the way to Heather's house."

"Mom, I promise you we are not planning to meet any boys on the way to Heather's house," Tia said, glad she didn't have to lie about that one. "We're growing up. We like the feeling of independence."

"I'll remember that, next time you want to be driven to the mall and you need your allowance." Lisa chuckled. "Okay, honey. Have a good time. See you tomorrow morning."

" 'Bye, Mom," Tia called.

" 'Bye, Dad," Tamera added.

They closed the front door.

"Phew. I thought we'd never get out of there," Tia said. "Talk about the Spanish Inquisition."

"I'm not too thrilled about turning down the chance for a ride," Tamera said. "I don't see what harm it would have done to go to Heather's house in a car."

"And suppose Heather had been watching for us and seen us arrive? That would have blown everything."

"I guess so," Tamera said. "But this activity is just a little too aerobic for me."

"I told you not to bring all those clothes," Tia said. "Look at that bag. It's about to burst."

"It takes a lot of props for a great actress like me

to look the part of a geek," Tamera said. "I like to be prepared for anything."

They walked on. "Is it always this far?" Tamera asked. "Are you sure we haven't missed the street?"

"It's not far really," Tia said. "I walk it all the time. It's just that the bags are getting heavy."

"No kidding," Tamera said. "My arm's about to fall off."

"Okay, this is Heather's street. The parting of the ways," Tia said, stopping at a corner under a street lamp. "Heather's house is the third on the right. The big Tudor with the tree in the front yard. Just try to say as little as possible, and don't blow it for me, okay?"

"I'll do my best," Tamera said. "It's not going to be easy. Geekiness doesn't come naturally to me. It's going to take an Oscar-winning performance."

"You can do it," Tia said. "Okay, this is where I transform from Tia to Super-Tia. Ready—trade!" She pulled off the Harvard sweatshirt while Tamera took off her velvet jacket. Solemnly they switched.

"I'll have to wait until I'm there to put on my makeup," Tia went on. "I can't see in the dark. So how do I look?"

"Good, I think," Tamera said. "Do I look geeky enough?"

"There's nothing geeky about a Harvard sweatshirt," Tia said. "I think it looks cool."

"It's not exactly me," Tamera said. "But I'll suffer."

"You can make it alone from here, right?" Tia asked. "You can carry both bags to Heather's house? I don't want to risk coming any closer in case she sees me."

"Fine. I'll just get a double hernia," Tamera said. "But I expect I'll manage. Go on then. Have a great time. Tell Clyde about me if you get the chance."

"Okay," Tia said. "Gotta go. 'Bye, Sis." She kissed Tamera on the cheek, then took a deep breath as she headed on down the street toward Clyde's house.

She could hear where the party was, even before she turned the corner to Clyde's street. And she could definitely tell right away which house was Clyde's. Music was blasting out of open windows. Cars were jammed into the driveway, and people were going in and out.

Tia stopped on the sidewalk, scared to go on for a second. She wanted *wild,* and this was definitely *wild.* She loved her music loud, but she had never been allowed to play it as loud as this. She could feel the beat throbbing through the soles of her shoes. I wonder why the neighbors don't complain, she thought.

Tia swallowed down her nervousness. This is it, she told herself. This is one of the great moments of your life—destiny with Clyde!

She took a deep breath and walked up the path to Clyde's front door. The door was half open, and Tia let herself in. There was hardly any light, and the whole house was vibrating to the beat of the rap number blasting from the stereo. What was usually the living room was now full of kids dancing. Tia stood there in the hallway, feeling awkward and not knowing what to do next.

Two girls passed her, looked at her, then did a double take. "Who are you?" one of them asked. Tia recognized the tall girl with the beaded braids who had nearly collided with Tamera in the school hall.

"I'm Tia," she mumbled. "I'm helping Clyde with his math. He invited me."

"Oh, yeah, right." The other girl laughed, digging the tall girl in the side. "You're the one who does Clyde's work for him. No wonder he's suddenly doing so well."

"I tutor him," Tia said defensively. "I explain and help him, but I don't exactly do his work."

"Oh, sure," the girl said with a knowing smile. "He told us how he can sweet-talk you into doing his homework for him. That boy is one smooth operator."

"Are you talking about me again behind my back?" Clyde asked, appearing suddenly between the two girls. "Hey, Tia. You made it. Guys, this is Tia, my own personal math whiz. I know all about parallelograms, thanks to her. And she writes a mean history paper, too, right Tia? Hey, Rocky," he called to a large boy in a dark sweater. "Get Tia something to drink."

"Uh, no, thanks, I'm not thirsty," Tia said, in

case he was talking about something stronger than a soda, but Rocky had disappeared.

In the background the music had changed to a slow, pulsating beat. "So, baby, how about you and me getting together for a little slow dancing," Clyde said.

Tia's heart did a complete flip-flop. She hadn't imagined it the other night. He really was interested in her. Then she heard the tall, beautiful girl saying, "Okay, if you really insist, I guess." And she saw that Clyde's arm was around her shoulder. Tia stood there watching as Clyde led the girl away through the crowd.

"Is, uh, she Clyde's girlfriend?" Tia asked the other girl, who was still standing beside her.

"Davina? She and Clyde are old friends," the girl said. "It's kind of on again, off again with them. Clyde never sticks to one girlfriend. He gets bored too easily." She stopped, looked at Tia's face, and then laughed. "You weren't hoping, were you? Oh, that's funny. Honey, between us girls, he's using you. He sees you as a way to get out of doing his homework, nothing more. And Clyde is always willing to do what it takes to get out of work."

"Me?" Tia tried to sound cool. "I'm not interested in Clyde. He's not my type at all. I just thought it would be fun to see what his parties are like."

"They're cool," the girls said. "Cool but crazy.

You wait until things get wild later on." She disappeared in the direction of the kitchen.

Tia looked around. She could hear shrieks of laughter coming from the kitchen. A group of kids passed her in the darkness.

"Did you know that Clyde invited that nerdy girl tonight?" one of them said. "You know, the one he pays to do his homework for him?"

"What did he do that for?" another voice asked.

"You know Clyde. Anything for a laugh. I wonder if she'll actually come?"

"Nah, she'd feel totally out of place, wouldn't she?"

They went on through to the living room, leaving Tia alone again.

Tia stood there, her cheeks burning, feeling embarrassed and angry. "I don't do his homework for him," she said out loud. But she realized that Clyde had sweet-talked her into doing a lot of his work—and then bragged about it.

They're right, she thought miserably. I should never have come. I don't belong here.

Chapter 12

෧෯

*T*amera tapped hesitantly on Heather's door. She had a bad feeling about this—her stomach felt as if she were about to take a math exam. Every time she turned over that math paper, she knew she was doomed—and that was exactly the way she was feeling now.

Heather opened the door, beaming at her. "Hi, Tia," she said, and threw her arms around Tamera in a big hug. "I'm so excited. Come on in," she went on.

Obstacle number one overcome, Tamera said to herself. At least Heather hadn't taken one look at her and screamed, "You're not Tia!"

Tamera staggered in with the two bags.

A gray-haired woman in a business suit appeared.

"Hello, Tia," she said.

"Hi, Mrs. Braunschweiger," Tamera blurted, hoping she had pronounced Heather's mother's name correctly. The woman smiled. So far, so good, Tamera said to herself.

"Go on up to Heather's room with that stuff," Heather's mother said.

Obstacle number two, Tamera said to herself. She had no idea where Heather's room was. She should have had Tia draw her a plan of the house.

"This stuff's heavy," she said, turning to Heather. "Will you give me a hand with it up the stairs?" She was just praying that Heather's bedroom was easy to find and not tucked away somewhere at the back of the house.

Heather picked up one of the bags. "Why did you bring so much stuff with you? It's only for one night," she said.

"Half of it is my sister Tamera's," Tamera said.

"She made you carry her bag over here?" Heather's mother asked. "That wasn't very nice of her."

"She's very irresponsible, Mom," Heather said. "She is exactly the opposite of you, isn't she, Tia? She doesn't take anything seriously."

"Hey, wait a second," Tamera interrupted. "She's just different, that's all. But she carried her own bag almost all the way here. She just was too shy to come up to the door right now."

Heather laughed. "What got into her? I wouldn't have called your sister shy. I'd have said she was the noisy extrovert. Remember how loudly she was laughing in the cafeteria that day?"

Tamera did remember. And if you knew what we were laughing about, she thought.

"Hurry up with those bags, girls," Heather's mother said. "Your father is waiting to leave. He wants to get a good seat at the lecture."

"After you," Tamera said, waving Heather ahead. She followed Heather up the stairs and into Heather's room. The moment she stepped inside, she just stood there, her mouth open. Heather's room was unlike any other bedroom she had been in. The entire ceiling was a glow-in-the-dark map of the heavens. A mobile of the planets hung from her light. There was a giant telescope at her window. Some sort of reptile was moving in a glass cage on her desk, and there was a whole wall of books. It was the room of Tamera's nightmares.

"Wow, this look's like a mad scientist's lab!" she couldn't help blurting out.

Heather looked at her strangely. "You've seen it before," she said. "What's so different about it tonight?"

"In this light," Tamera said hastily. "I mean it looks kind of spooky in the dark."

"I love it," Heather said. "I love lying in bed and looking at the stars. We can have fun later when you sleep over. We'll have a competition to see who can identify the most constellations."

"I can hardly wait," Tamera said. "Is that your

mom calling us? We'd better go. We don't want to keep your dad waiting."

Keep quiet, Tamera, she warned herself as they went back downstairs. Just don't say a word and you'll be okay.

"Here they are. Splendid. Splendid," Heather's father said, clapping his hands and leaping up from his chair. "Off we go then. It's going to be fun, isn't it, girls?"

"Right," Tamera mumbled, because he was looking straight at her.

She thought he looked like a cartoon of a mad professor. He had a lot of wiry gray hair that stood out from his head and very thick, heavy-rimmed glasses.

Tamera climbed into the Volvo station wagon next to Heather, and they took off. She hoped that Heather's father would put on some music so that they wouldn't have to talk, but he didn't.

"So, Tia. I understand you're a big fan of Galileo?" Heather's father asked.

Tamera's mind raced. "Is he a baseball player?" she asked.

The other occupants of the car laughed.

"I meant the space probe," Heather's father said. "You know, the one that's responsible for sending back all this data."

"Oh, *that* Galileo," Tamera said. "I thought you meant Joe Galileo. Doesn't he play for the Cubs?"

Tamera could feel Heather looking at her. "I

didn't think you liked baseball," she said. "In fact, you told me that it was the most boring game on earth."

"I *don't* like it," Tamera said hastily. "But I hear about it on the news."

I am heading for a mega disaster, she told herself. I put my foot in everything I say.

It was too late now to claim she had laryngitis and the doctor had forbidden her to speak. Besides, Heather's mother was so health conscious that she might have sent her home again. The drive to the lecture seemed to take forever. Tamera was sure they must have driven clear across Detroit and still they kept on driving. She began to wonder if the lecture was actually in Chicago, or even New York City.

At last they turned into a parking lot. Tamera heaved a big sigh of relief as she walked beside Heather into a lecture hall.

At least the next part will be easy, she thought. All I have to do is sit and listen. Just as long as they don't quiz me on the lecture afterward.

The lecturer was introduced and began to talk. He asked for the room to be darkened and started showing slides on a screen behind him. "It has long been maintained that the nature of the cloud cover on Jupiter was largely composed of blah, blah blah . . ." A slide of mustard yellow swirling nothingness appeared on the screen. Tamera shifted in her seat. The chairs were hard and uncomfortable.

The lecturer droned on and on. More and more

slides came onto the screen. Orangy clouds, pinkish clouds, pink and orange clouds together. The room was getting stuffy. Tamera closed her eyes. Let it be over soon, she begged. She could imagine what Tia was doing right now. She tried to picture herself at Clyde's party. She could see Tia dancing with Clyde. If I were there I'd be able to show them, she thought angrily. I dance way better than Tia. In her mind she put herself into Tia's place. The music changed to a slow dance, and she was in Clyde's arms. He was holding her tightly and smiling down into her eyes. She felt herself floating until suddenly Clyde let go of her.

"Ow!" she cried as she hit the hard, cold floor. She opened her eyes and looked around. She was on the floor of the lecture hall. She had just fallen off her chair.

"Tia, are you all right?" Heather asked, dropping to her knees beside Tamera.

"Yeah, I'm fine," Tamera said, wishing she could die of embarrassment. "Stupid chair. I was just trying to get comfortable." She sat down again, and this time she propped her eyelids open with her fingers, in case they felt like closing again.

"Wasn't that stimulating?" Heather's father asked them as the lights came on and the lecturer bowed to applause. "What wonderful discoveries."

"Yeah, that Galileo guy sure took some good snapshots," Tamera said.

Heather giggled nervously. "Tia, the probe was unmanned," she said.

"I knew that," Tamera said hastily.

"How about we stop off and get a snack on the way home?" Heather's mother said. "I expect you girls are hungry after sitting for so long."

"Good idea," Heather's father said. "What do you feel like, Tia?"

"A foot-long hot dog with the works!" Tamera blurted out before she remembered.

"A hot dog?" Heather's mother sounded shocked.

"I meant a veggie dog," Tamera said quickly. "Isn't there a place around here that does veggie dogs? In that case, forget it. Ice cream would do fine. Did I say ice cream? I meant frozen yogurt . . . nonfat frozen yogurt . . . frozen bean curd . . ."

"Tia, what's with you?" Heather whispered. "You're acting so strangely tonight."

"I'm just nervous," Tamera said. "I'm always nervous when I'm out with friends' parents."

"I'd go for hot chocolate and doughnuts," Heather said to her parents.

"Hot chocolate and doughnuts. Good idea," Tamera said, glad it wasn't something nonfat, nonmeat, and nontaste.

They stopped off at the DonutWorks and had enormous apple fritters and hot chocolate. Tamera ate in silence.

"Are you always this quiet, Tia?" Heather's father asked.

"I'm not very good at eating and talking at the same time," Tamera said. She made her doughnut last until the very last second, while Heather and her parents argued about the lecture. She imagined her dad and Lisa fighting over whether Jupiter could support life and if the life would be carbon based.

I'm glad I live where I do, she thought. And I'm glad Heather is Tia's friend, not mine.

As she thought this, she realized something—she had been jealous of Tia for having a best friend and not including her. She began to understand that she and Tia might be sisters, but they liked different things. There was no reason for them to have the same friends and hang out together all the time.

Half an hour later they were back at Heather's house, and she was putting on Tia's flannel pajamas with the hearts on them. Another hour before Tia shows up, she thought, glancing at her watch. I just hope I can hold out that long.

"So what do you want to do until your sister gets here?" Heather asked. "How about a game of chess?"

"Chess?" Tia had tried to teach her once, without much success. "I'm not really in a chess kind of mood," she said. "Why don't we just watch some TV?"

"TV? I don't think there's anything good on the Discovery Channel tonight," Heather said.

"Some music then?" Tamera suggested. "Why don't we put on a CD?"

"Okay, you select," Heather said, handing Tamera a box of CDs. Tamera started looking through them. Mozart. Bach. Rimsky-Korsakov.

They both jumped at a tapping noise at the window.

"What was that?" Heather asked.

"Someone's outside your window."

"There can't be. We're on the second floor."

Tamera went over to the window and opened it cautiously. She looked around and then gasped as she saw a face, peering up at her from the garage roof below. "Roger, what are you doing?" she demanded.

"Who is it?" Heather asked, leaning out next to Tamera.

"It's Roger, the little creep," Tamera said. "My neighbor. I expect it's his idea of fun to crash a girls' sleepover. But he's just leaving, aren't you, Roger?"

"Listen, I don't risk life and limb without a very good reason," Roger said. "That drainpipe was very unstable, but I happen to care about you and your sister, and I'm not about to let you get into trouble."

"What are you talking about?" Tamera asked.

"I was just at Clyde's house," Roger said.

"You were at Clyde's party? He invited you and not me?"

"No, he didn't invite me," Roger said. "I heard he was having a party, so I thought I'd go snoop. I heard his parties were pretty wild. I thought I might get some ideas for picking up chicks."

"Huh. Some chance," Tamera said.

"Anyway. I snooped on his party, and you'll never guess who I saw there. Your sister, Tia!"

"So what? I knew she was there."

"Tamera—you let your sister go to that party? What kind of sister are you?"

"Clyde Hemming's parties are cool!"

"Clyde Hemming's parties get raided by the cops!" Roger said.

"Wait a minute," Heather interrupted. "What is he talking about?"

"Her sister, Tia, is at this party that is too wild for her," Roger said. "I thought of going to her folks, but then I thought that I didn't want to get Tia in trouble."

"You mean get Tamera in trouble," Heather said. "This is Tia."

"You think I don't know the difference between these two?" Roger laughed. "You're looking at a guy who has dated both of them, right, Tamera?"

"Not exactly," Tamera said coldly.

Heather was glaring at her. "You're not Tia?" she demanded. "Is this some sort of joke?"

"It's a long story," Tamera said. "I'll explain later."

"You'd better come with me right away and get Tia out of there before the cops come," Roger insisted. "I don't think her mom would be too pleased if she had to pick her up at the juvenile detention center."

"No kidding," Tamera said. "I'll slip on some clothes and meet you outside, Roger."

She started pulling on her jeans over her pajamas. Heather started dressing, too.

"You don't have to come," Tamera said.

"You bet I do," Heather said. "How could she do this to me? I'm not going to let her get away with this." She struggled into a second sneaker. "We'd better go out through the back door. That way we won't have to pass my parents," she said. "Just don't make any noise. I don't want to get in trouble."

Tamera followed her down the stairs and out through the kitchen door. Then they sped around the house. Roger was waiting by the front gate.

"I just hope we're not too late," he said. "Come on, run!"

Chapter 13

Tia was feeling cold and miserable. It had taken her only five minutes to decide that she didn't belong at the party. Everyone there thought she was a joke—Clyde's tame smart person who did his homework for him. She should have realized that Clyde had way too big an ego to admit he was being tutored. So he'd made it sound as if he was the smart one and he had conned her into doing his work—which was partly true, Tia thought, her toes curling with embarrassment. Why had she let herself be swept away by those gorgeous long eyelashes? Didn't she pride herself on being a smart, sensible person? Yet she had been taken in by Clyde, like every other girl, and he had only invited her as a joke, she knew that now.

After the first few minutes he hadn't noticed her all evening. In fact, nobody had paid any attention to her, except for the annoying Rocky, who had tried to flirt with her and wouldn't take no for an answer. And it only took her a few minutes to discover something else, too—she didn't really want to get to know Clyde and his friends. They were not her kind of people, and this was definitely not her kind of party!

She really wanted to go home, but that would have blown everything and probably would end up getting both her and Tamera in trouble. In the end she had hidden out in the garden, wishing that it was time to go to Heather's house. The minutes ticked by painfully slowly. She guessed that Heather would be home by ten, but she couldn't show up there much before eleven. Nobody left cool parties at ten o'clock. If she showed up too early, Tamera would know that she'd had a bad time. And she couldn't let Tamera know the truth, at least not right away. That would prove everything that Tamera had said—that she didn't belong with cool kids.

Tia sniffed back a tear. She had really wanted to prove to Tamera that she was the cool, popular twin. Instead it looked as if she'd be the twin who came down with pneumonia from hiding in a cold garden.

Tia stiffened as she heard voices coming closer down the street.

"We're in luck. There's no sign of the cops yet."

"How are we going to get her out of there without embarrassing her?"

"Tell her a family emergency has come up."

Tia recognized those voices. One of them sounded suspiciously like her sister, and the other was unmistakably Roger. She peeked around the bush, and there they were, running toward her. Tia fought back her desire to rush out and throw her arms around Tamera. Instead she realized she was mad. They thought she needed rescuing—they didn't think she was smart enough to make her own decisions. Well, she'd show them.

She ducked down behind the bush. "Oh, Clyde," she said. "I'm glad I'm out here all alone with you. What? Sure, I'd love another—"

"Tia!" Tamera burst into the front yard. "Come out of there this second. I'm taking you home right now."

Tia emerged from the bush.

"And tell that creep Clyde he should be ashamed of himself," Tamera went on. "You hear that, Clyde Hemming? I thought you were cute and cool once, but I've changed my mind."

A grin spread across Tia's face. "You're wasting your energy," she said. "He's not there."

"Then who is?"

"Nobody. I was out here all alone," she said.

"Then why did you say that stuff and get me worried?" Tamera demanded.

"To give you a scare," Tia said. "You should

know me better than that, Tamera. You know I'm not the kind of person who would do stuff just because other kids were doing it."

"How do I know that?" Tamera said angrily. "You were boasting about you and Clyde."

"Only because you called me a geek."

"Only because you were acting so superior at home and making me feel small."

"Me?" Tia demanded. "Making you feel small?"

"Yeah. Everyone was making a fuss over you," Tamera said. " 'Oh, Tia's so smart. Why can't you be more like your sister, Tamera? How come you're so dumb and she's so smart?' What do you think that felt like, huh?"

"You could have told me," Tia said. "I had no idea you were feeling like that. I guess I was enjoying being a celebrity for the first time in my life. I didn't realize it was making you feel bad."

"The only way to make myself feel better was to put you down," Tamera said. "I started calling you a geek, and I guess it worked."

"It really hurt me," Tia said. "That's why this party was so important to me. Everyone would think I was cool if I hung out with Clyde Hemming. Only it didn't take me long to realize that I didn't want to hang out with Clyde Hemming. I wanted to go back to you guys."

"So what were you doing out in the bushes?" Roger asked.

"Waiting until it was time to go home," Tia said.

"I couldn't leave too early, or you guys might have suspected something."

"Yeah, I might have suspected that you were playing a trick on me," Heather said.

Tia hadn't noticed her until now, standing back in the shadows. "Heather, what are you doing here?"

"Waiting to tell you what I think of you," Heather said. "Some friend you are. You lied to me, Tia. You played a mean trick on me."

"I'm sorry," Tia said. "I only did it because I didn't want to let you down. I knew you were looking forward to going to the lecture with me."

"So you sent *her* instead?" Heather demanded. "I thought you'd flipped out, Tia. Your sister thought Galileo was a baseball player, and she fell asleep and slid off her chair. I couldn't believe you'd turned into such a moron."

"Hey, don't call me a moron," Tamera said at the same moment as Tia said, "Don't call my sister a moron."

"Well, she is," Heather said. "She hasn't got a clue about anything. Talk about airhead. And I guess you're just as bad if you'd prefer that party to me."

"Thanks a lot. And if you really want to know, I didn't really prefer the party to you," Tia said angrily. "I just had to show Tamera that I was cooler than she was."

"Why should you care what your sister thought

about you?" Heather asked. "You know you're a smart person and a fun person. It shouldn't matter what anyone else thought of you."

"But it does," Tia said. "I felt terrible when Tamera laughed at me. It seemed like all the brains in the world wouldn't make up for being someone other people thought was weird."

"I don't understand you," Heather said. "I don't care what anyone else thinks of me."

"But I do," Tia said. "I want to be liked. I want to be popular. I want to have fun in high school."

"Just stick with me, baby," Roger said, moving close to Tia. "I'll show you what a good time's really like."

"Euuww, get away from me," Tia said.

"Don't be too mean to Roger," Tamera said. "He was the one who wanted to rescue you. He came to find me after he snooped on the party and saw you there."

"I saved you, baby," Roger said. "I'm a hero."

"Don't speak too soon," Tamera said as the wail of a siren rose on the wind. "Here come the cops. Quick, let's get out of here."

They fled down the block as flashing lights turned into the other end of the street.

"There's a police car coming this way, too," Tia wailed. "Quick. Hide."

They ducked behind a garden wall and waited, holding their breath as the car raced past, coming to a halt outside Clyde's house. They watched as the officers moved toward Clyde's front door.

"Now," Tia whispered. "We can sneak around the corner and get back to Heather's house. Come on, run for it."

They sprinted down the block. Waiting at the end of the street was a long white limo, blocking their way back to Heather's house.

"Oh, no!" Tamera wailed.

The limo window slid silently open.

"Hi, girls," Ray said calmly. "Do you mind telling me what you're doing?"

"Uh . . . late-night jogging?" Tamera suggested.

"You know you're not allowed out wandering the streets at ten-thirty at night," Ray said. "You'd better get in the car right now. I'll drop off your friend, and then you're going straight home, both of you."

"But, Daddy, we're supposed to be spending the night at Heather's house," Tamera said.

"Her parents will worry," Tia added.

"Her parents didn't seem to think there was anything wrong in letting you girls go out alone," Ray said.

"We, uh, snuck out," Tamera said. "Heather's parents don't know we've gone."

"And it wasn't Heather's fault, either," Tia added.

"Or mine," Roger chimed in. "Do I get a ride, too, Mr. Campbell? I'm too young to be out walking the streets alone at night."

"Okay, Roger. You can come up front with me,"

Ray said. "You girls, hop in the back. I'll tell Heather's parents that I've changed my mind about the sleepover, and I'm sure Lisa will agree with me when she hears."

"Does she have to hear, Ray?" Tia asked, wincing.

"I'd like to know exactly what you girls were doing," Ray said. "I hear police sirens, I go to look, and the next thing I know, I see my daughter and her sister running away as fast as they can. Now, what do you suppose I think about that?"

"That we were in the wrong place at the wrong time?" Tamera said weakly.

"Honestly, Mr. Campbell, we weren't doing anything wrong," Heather spoke up. "We were just checking out a party—just looking, from the outside. Then we heard the sirens and thought it might be wise to move on."

"I see," Ray said.

Tamera looked in surprise at Heather. "All right, Heather," she whispered.

"And I take it your parents don't even know that you're out?" Ray said.

"No, sir. We snuck out the back way," Heather said.

"Heather, I'm pretty sure that you weren't the one who had this crazy idea," Ray said. "I'd like to bet it was my daughter who put you up to this, and I'll talk to her in the morning. She might find she's grounded until she turns twenty-one. But I don't want to get you in trouble, so I'm going to drop you off and let you sneak back in the way you came."

"Thanks, Mr. Campbell," Heather said.

"And, Tia, I don't think you would have been the one who wanted to check out a wild party," Ray went on. "So I won't say anything to your mother until I've found out the truth tomorrow."

Tamera glared at Tia. Tia said nothing.

"This is my house," Heather said. The car pulled up. The girls got out.

"See you in the morning, Daddy," Tamera said in a small voice. " 'Bye."

The car drove off. Tamera turned on Tia. "Thanks for nothing, Miss Goody-Goody! 'It couldn't have been you who did anything wrong, Miss Perfect, because you are a member of the Einsteinettes. It has to be my dumb daughter here!' "

"I'll explain in the morning if you want me to." Tia was twisting her hair nervously. "I just didn't think it would be very smart to go into details tonight when he was mad." She looked hopefully at Tamera. "Do you really think we'll be in big trouble for this?"

"Running away from a wild party and a police car in the middle of the night? Why should our parents worry about that?"

"Heather came up with a very reasonable explanation," Tia said. "I think we should stick to it. We heard the noise of the party, we went to look, the police came, we ran. That doesn't sound too terrible, does it? I'm sure my mom wouldn't blow her top over that. She might get a little mad, she might ground me for a week, but it wouldn't be the convent with the ten-foot wall."

"I don't think my dad is going to forgive and forget that easily," Tamera said. "And if I'm in trouble, you're in trouble. I'm not being the fall guy. I already spent a whole evening in the company of geeks for you."

"Okay, okay, I promise I'll explain everything to our parents tomorrow. But wait a second—I only went to the party because you called me a geek!"

"And I only called you a geek because you were acting so stuck up and hanging out with Heather and leaving me out."

Tamera's words hung in the crisp night air.

"So that's what started all this?" Tia exclaimed. "You were jealous?"

"Why would I be jealous of a geek hanging out with another geek?"

"Hey, I resent being insulted like this," Heather interrupted.

"Shut up, Heather, we're fighting, don't interrupt," the girls said at the identical moment. They glared at each other, then their mouths began to twitch and they started to laugh.

There were more sirens blaring through the night.

"Okay, I was jealous," Tamera admitted at last. "I didn't want you to be the star in the family, and

I didn't want you to have a best friend and leave me out, either."

"But, Tamera, just because we're sisters doesn't have to mean we like the same things, or have the same friends," Tia said.

"I know that," Tamera said. "You and I have totally different tastes when it comes to interests and to friends."

"Are you guys going to stand there in the street all night?" Heather demanded. "Tamera, you and I will have to sneak in the way we came and then Tia can ring the front doorbell and we'll answer it."

"Good thinking, Heather," Tamera said. "You know what? You're okay. You did some quick thinking back there in the limo. I'm sorry I called you a geek."

"It's okay," Heather said.

"Now you can say you're sorry you called me an airhead," Tamera said.

Tia started laughing. "But, Tamera, you *are* an airhead sometimes. Imagine falling off your chair at a lecture. How embarrassing."

"If you'd been at that lecture, you'd have fallen off your chair, too," Tamera said. "Talk about boring. Falling off my chair was the one exciting thing that happened to me all evening."

"I thought it was a great lecture," Heather said. "Very stimulating."

"Like I said, different strokes for different folks,"

Tamera said with a grin to Tia. "I'm glad I don't have to spend any more evenings like this."

"Me, too," Tia said. "I'm glad I never have to go to a party like that again."

"It's a pity Clyde Hemming turned out to be such a loser," Tamera said. "He was so cute."

"He was certainly cute," Tia agreed, "but you wouldn't have wanted him as a boyfriend. Talk about an overinflated ego! That boy thought he was all that."

"Who needs Clyde Hemming? We can find ourselves nice, ordinary guys to take to Sarah's party," Tamera said.

"Where?" Tia asked. "The party's next week."

"There's always Roger," Tamera suggested.

"If anyone gets Roger, it will be me," Tia said. "I was the one he came to rescue, remember?"

"But I was the one he liked first."

"But he fell in love with my superior brain."

"He'd have more fun with me."

"You two," Heather said, stepping in between them. "Do you have to fight over everything?"

Tia and Tamera looked at each other. "It's okay. We could always share him," Tia said.

"My turn first," Tamera said, laughing. She threw her arm around Tia's shoulder as they walked up to Heather's front door.

About the Author

Janet Quin-Harkin has written over fifty books for teenagers, including the best-seller *Ten-Boy Summer*. She is the author of several popular series: TGIF!, Friends, Heartbreak Café, Senior Year, and The Boyfriend Club. She has also written several romances.

Ms. Quin-Harkin lives with her husband in San Rafael, California. She has four children. In addition to writing books, she teaches creative writing at a nearby college.

FOR MORE LAUGHS

TUNE IN TO

Sister Sister

ON THE
WB TELEVISION
NETWORK

THE **WB**

TELEVISION NETWORK

(PLEASE CHECK LOCAL LISTINGS FOR DAY AND TIME)